EMILY'S WORLD
The New Jersey Shore in 1925

GANGSTERS AT THE
GRAND ATLANTIC

⚬❧

by
Sarah Masters Buckey

American Girl ®

HISTORY MYSTERIES

Visit our Web site at **americangirl.com**

Printed in the United States of America.
03 04 05 06 07 08 RRD 10 9 8 7 6 5 4 3 2 1

History Mysteries® and American Girl®
are registered trademarks of Pleasant Company.

PERMISSIONS & PICTURE CREDITS
The following individuals and organizations have generously given permission
to reprint illustrations contained in "A Peek into the Past": pp. 158–159 — flapper in
bathing suit, © Underwood & Underwood/CORBIS; telephone operators, Corbis;
suffrage buttons, National Museum of American History, Smithsonian Institution,
Behring Center; police emptying beer barrels, © Underwood & Underwood/CORBIS;
pp. 160–161 — Al Capone, © Underwood & Underwood/CORBIS; couple by radio, CORBIS;
mah-jongg tiles, courtesy Erin Falligant; pp. 162–163 — dancers, © Hulton Archive/Getty Images;
movie poster, Hershenson-Allen Archive, West Plains, MO; Laura LaPlante and her sister
with auto, © Hulton Archive/Getty Images; Franklin Roosevelt, FDR Library;
flappers at beach, *National Police Gazette*, New York Public Library.

Cover and Map Illustrations: Douglas Fryer
Line Art: Greg Dearth

Library of Congress Cataloging-in-Publication Data

Buckey, Sarah Masters, 1955–
Gangsters at the Grand Atlantic / by Sarah Masters Buckey. — 1st ed.
p. cm. — (History mysteries ; 20)
"American girl."
Summary: In 1925, after witnessing the violent actions of some gangsters, twelve-year-old Emily
accompanies her older sister on a trip to a luxurious hotel on the New Jersey shore but worries
that the gangsters have come to the same hotel. Includes historical notes on the time period.

ISBN 1-58485-720-X — ISBN 1-58485-719-6 (pbk.)
[1. Sisters—Fiction. 2. Gangsters—Fiction. 3. Beaches—Fiction. 4. Hotels—Fiction.
5. New Jersey—History—20th century—Fiction. 6. Mystery and detective stories.]
I. Title. II. Series.
PZ7.B87983 Gan 2002   [Fic]—dc21   2002071701

To J.J., A.W., and J.M.
With love, always

TABLE OF CONTENTS

CHAPTER I

THE INVITATION

Twelve-year-old Emily Scott opened the door labeled "Exit." She hoped to see stairs that would lead her from the basement of the Philadelphia Museum of Art up to the museum's first floor. Instead, she found a pitch-black hall that smelled strongly of fresh paint.

That can't be the way out, she thought, quickly closing the door. *But where should I go now?*

Most of the huge new Philadelphia Museum of Art was still under construction. Only a few temporary galleries were open, and they were all in the basement. But the basement was pleasantly cool—much nicer than the crowded dress shops where Emily's older sister, Dorothy, had wanted to spend the afternoon.

"Don't talk to strangers," Dorothy had instructed when she left Emily at the museum door. "Don't be late to meet me. And *don't* tell Mother I let you stay here by yourself!"

Emily secretly wished that Dorothy would have wanted

to stay with her. Still, Emily had enjoyed the paintings, and her afternoon had gone well—until she'd left the galleries to go to the ladies' room. On her way back to the exhibits, she must have made a wrong turn. Now she was in a part of the museum she'd never seen before.

She walked farther down the windowless hall. The walls were rough and unpainted, and the only light came from a bare bulb in the ceiling. She turned a corner and saw a jumble of tools and lumber. But there was no pounding of hammers or shouts of men working. *The workmen must have gone home,* she realized.

Her hands started to sweat. She was supposed to meet Dorothy in front of the museum at five o'clock. *What time is it now?* Emily wondered. *And how do I get out of here?*

She closed her eyes. If she could picture something in her mind, she could usually recall it exactly. Now if she could just remember the hall to the galleries ...

The tromp of heavy boots echoed through the basement. A man wearing a carpenter's leather apron approached from the other end of the hallway. "Is there a problem, miss?" he asked.

Emily bit her lip. She couldn't possibly tell this stranger that she'd gone to the ladies' room, then been unable to find her way back to the galleries. All she could do was nod.

"I bet you're wanting to get back to the pictures, eh?" he said kindly.

Emily nodded again. Her face grew hot with embarrassment.

"This way," he said, gesturing for Emily to follow. He led her back down the corridor and through a maze of dark halls. Then he opened the door to the gallery. Emily blinked against the sudden brightness. A familiar voice cried out, "Where *were* you?"

Emily turned and saw her sister hurrying toward her. Dorothy's slim black heels clicked sharply against the gallery floor. The carpenter tipped his cap and explained that Emily had been lost in the basement. "My little sister is always getting lost," Dorothy told him. "Thank you for finding her."

The carpenter tipped his cap again and was gone. Dorothy glared at her sister. "I rushed from my shopping to meet you. Look at the time now!"

Emily glanced at the clock on the wall. It was ten minutes past five. *Uh-oh!*

"I waited outside till the museum started to close," Dorothy continued. "Then I came in to look for you. The guards told me everyone had left—but I was sure you must be here somewhere. I know how scatterbrained you are!"

"I'm not scatterbrained," Emily protested. "And I'm not always getting lost—why did you tell the man that?"

"Because it's true," said Dorothy. "I remember when you got lost in Rittenhouse Square. Mother and I were only a few yards away, but you thought we were gone forever."

"I was six years old then!" Emily defended herself. "Besides, this was different. I was going to find my way out!"

"Sure you were," Dorothy said sarcastically. She took her sister's arm. "Let's go. If we hurry, we can still be home before Mother."

As they left the building, Emily saw her sister and herself reflected in the museum's windows. Eighteen-year-old Dorothy was the kind of modern girl everyone called a "flapper." Her dark brown hair was cut in a fashionable chin-length bob, and it swung as she walked. She was wearing a tiny black hat and a sleeveless black-and-white–striped dress that stopped daringly at her knees. The dress looked expensive, but Emily knew that Dorothy had copied the pattern from a magazine and sewn it herself.

Emily was almost as tall as her sister, but while Dorothy was stylishly slim, Emily was just skinny. Her white blouse and blue skirt drooped on her thin frame. Emily often begged her mother for a short haircut like Dorothy's, but Mother insisted she keep her braids. "You're a schoolgirl, and you should look like a schoolgirl," Mother always said. "When you're a college girl like Dorothy, you can look like a college girl."

Now Emily glanced enviously at her sister. Even on this sticky summer day, Dorothy's bobbed hair stayed smooth, while Emily's braids frizzled in the humidity. *I'll never be as pretty as Dorothy,* Emily thought. *No matter how old I get.*

The sun beat down as the girls headed to their trolley

stop. When they reached the corner, several people were already clustered at the stop. Emily peered down the street. Behind the delivery carts pulled by sweating horses and the motorcars spouting smoke, she glimpsed the green trolley. "Thank heavens we didn't miss it," Dorothy said as they lined up to get onboard. "Emily, you'd better get our nickels."

Emily dug into the pocket of her skirt. It was empty. She felt a twinge of dread. "Uh, Dot..." she began.

"Call me Dorothy, not Dot," her sister reminded her. "Hurry! We need two nickels."

The trolley clanged its bell at the stop. As the girls moved up in line, Emily whispered, "I think I left the money in the museum."

"What!" Dorothy exclaimed. A few people turned and stared, and Dorothy lowered her voice. "That was our last quarter! I said you could buy one postcard, but we needed money for trolley fare. Don't you remember?"

"Yes," Emily confessed. "When I went to the ladies' room, I put the postcard and our nickels by the sink. I must have left them there."

Dorothy looked back toward the museum. It loomed in the distance like a huge Greek temple. "The museum is closed," she said. "It's too late to go back."

Emily nodded miserably. "I know. I'm sorry!"

"You'd lose your head if it wasn't attached!" Dorothy said, exasperated.

They had reached the front of the line. "Fare, please!" called the conductor. He held out his hand. Patches of color rose in Dorothy's cheeks. "We've changed our minds," she told the conductor. "We'll walk."

For Emily, the long walk home was horrible. The streets smelled of tar and horse manure, and waves of heat floated from the pavement. Worst of all, Dorothy hardly spoke. She strode ahead, her mouth drawn in an angry line.

I wish she'd yell at me and get it over with, Emily thought.

Emily remembered how, when they were younger, she and Dorothy could talk about anything. That was when they had lived on a farm, and Father was the minister for a small church. Mother had played organ for the church and painted pictures of the Pennsylvania countryside.

Emily and Dorothy had loved their farm and all their pets: a small dachshund named Homer and a huge sheepdog named Prince, three farm cats—Mack, Jack, and Josie— and a goose named Pepper.

Few neighbors had lived nearby, so the sisters had spent most of their time with each other. They'd done chores together, played together, and shared a bedroom together. Mother had even sewn them matching dresses. "Dot and Em are like two peas in a pod," their father used to say fondly.

When Emily was five, Father had been called to serve as an army chaplain during the Great War. He had died on a battlefield, just before the war ended. After Father's death, Mother had struggled to keep their farm in the country, but the family's bills had piled up.

Finally, Mother had admitted defeat. She had taken a job teaching music and art at Miss Andrews' Academy for Girls in Philadelphia. The family had moved to an apartment near the school, but the city was no place for farm animals. All of their pets, except Homer, had been given away.

For Emily, the move had been wrenching. In her city neighborhood, there were no hills for sledding or ponds for swimming. She could no longer play outside by herself. ("It's too dangerous," Mother said.) She wasn't even allowed to swim in the public pool. ("There's too much risk of catching polio," Mother said.)

Emily had ached for her old home and their quiet life in the country. Most of all, she'd missed her animals. But Dorothy had comforted her. "Mother and I will always be with you, Em," Dorothy had promised. "No matter what."

A year ago, though, Dorothy had won a scholarship to Vassar College in New York. Emily had tried to share her sister's excitement about college, but she'd missed Dorothy terribly. Throughout the school year, she'd looked forward to having Dorothy home for the summer.

Now, however, things were not at all the way Emily had hoped they would be. *She never calls me Em anymore; it's just Emily. And now she's Dorothy, never Dot. And she's bossier than Mother. I wish—*

Dorothy interrupted her thoughts. "We'll take a short-cut here," she announced, motioning toward an alley.

"Are you sure?" Emily asked. "Mother says—"

"Never mind that now," Dorothy ordered. "We're in a hurry. Come on."

The long alley smelled like rotting vegetables. When the girls emerged at the other end, they were on a side street where wet laundry flapped from apartment windows and all the buildings had peeling paint. Several teenage boys sat on a stoop, smoking cigarettes and laughing.

As Dorothy led the way down the sidewalk, the sisters passed a boarded-up building that looked as if it had once been a restaurant. Emily saw a sign nailed across the door: *CLOSED BY ORDER OF FEDERAL AGENTS.*

"What does that mean?" she asked Dorothy.

"It was probably a speakeasy," Dorothy said. She looked over at Emily. "You *do* know what a speakeasy is, don't you?"

"A place that sells illegal drinks, like beer or whiskey?" Emily ventured.

Dorothy nodded. "That's right. Federal agents must've raided it. They probably arrested the owners—and maybe the customers. Then they shut it down, but—"

Suddenly, a shiny black Stutz motorcar screeched to a halt beside the girls. Four flashily dressed men were in the car. One called to Dorothy, "Hey, beautiful, want a ride?"

"Ignore them!" Dorothy whispered. She grabbed Emily's elbow and walked even faster than before.

The men drove slowly beside them, whistling and calling out. Emily kept her eyes on the ground and walked as quickly as she could. Soon the girls reached a busy intersection. They turned north, but the Stutz followed.

Dorothy clenched her jaw. "When I say 'Go,' we'll run across!" she whispered to Emily. Dorothy looked for a break in the cars. "Go!"

Dodging behind the Stutz, the sisters plunged across to the opposite sidewalk. Now they were walking against traffic, and the Stutz could no longer trail them. With a honk, the men sped off.

"Thank heavens they're gone," Dorothy exclaimed. "They looked like gangsters."

Emily watched the shiny black car drive off into the distance. "Where do gangsters get the money for a fancy car like that?"

"Bootlegging liquor, probably," said Dorothy. "Prohibition made liquor illegal, but lots of places still sell it—like that speakeasy we saw. And speakeasies buy their liquor from men like that."

Emily was glad when they finally turned the corner onto Gardner Avenue. It was a quiet street sandwiched between well-to-do neighborhoods on one side and crowded working-class areas on the other. Narrow three-story buildings lined the pavement, and elm trees shaded the sidewalk.

The Scotts lived at 14B Gardner Avenue, just above Florio's Foods. Mr. Florio, an elderly widower, owned the

building. He lived alone in an apartment on the third floor
and kept his small grocery store on the ground level. Stairs
on the left side of the building led up to the Scotts' apartment on the second floor.

Dorothy unlocked the side entrance, but Emily paused
before going upstairs. She opened the door that connected
the apartment entrance to the store. "Hello, Mr. Florio!"

Mr. Florio looked up, and a smile wrinkled his face. He
was a small man and his back was hunched by age, but his
brown eyes were cheerful. "Hello, girls!" he greeted them.
"Your mama's looking for you. She was worried 'cause you
were late."

"Uh-oh," Dorothy muttered.

"And, Dorothy," Mr. Florio continued, "you got a
telegram today. I gave it to your mama."

Dorothy brightened. "Really!" she exclaimed. "I wonder
who it's from!" She ran upstairs, and Emily followed. As
they walked in the door, Homer jumped up, barking joyfully. Emily knelt to pat the excited dachshund. Dorothy
rushed past her.

"Mother!" she called. "We're home."

Mother came out of the kitchen, wiping her hands on
her apron. She was a slim, graceful woman with blue eyes
and long dark hair swept up in a bun. "Where have you
been, girls? I expected you earlier."

Emily held her breath. How much would Dorothy
tell Mother?

But all Dorothy said was, "We were at the museum till it closed, and then we decided to walk home." She paused and looked around the entryway. "Mr. Florio said there's a telegram for me . . ."

"It's on the piano, dear," said Mother.

Dorothy hurried into the small living room, grabbed the telegram, and ripped it open. Her eyes scanned it quickly. Then she whooped with joy. "My friend Bitsy Brewster is spending next week at the Jersey Shore. She and her mother are staying at the Grand Atlantic Hotel. And Bitsy wants me to join them!"

"Next week?" Mother asked doubtfully.

"Yes!" Dorothy exclaimed. "She says to come Monday!"

Mother frowned. "I'm sorry, dear, but that's out of the question. My classes are finished for the year, but I must work next week to prepare graduating girls for their music recitals. I need you to stay home with Emily."

Emily watched the joy drain from her sister's face like water sucked out of a washtub. *Dot doesn't want to stay home with me,* thought Emily with a stab of pain.

"Mother, I'm twelve years old. I can stay home alone," Emily offered. "Dot—I mean Dorothy—can go with her friend."

Mother looked from Emily to Dorothy. Then she pulled a dime from her apron. "Emily, dear, go downstairs to Mr. Florio's store. We need a quart of milk for dinner."

Emily took the dime and stepped out of the apartment.

As she stood on the landing, she heard her sister pleading. *"Please* let me go, Mother! Emily will be all right by herself for a few hours during the day. When I was twelve, I stayed home alone sometimes."

"We lived in the country then," Mrs. Scott reminded her. "The city isn't safe for a girl Emily's age. Besides, you've always been mature for your age, Dorothy, while Emily..." Mother's voice trailed off.

Emily's face burned. She hated being thought of as a baby! Yet she didn't want Dorothy to go away, either. *This is the worst summer ever,* she thought as she clumped downstairs.

Mr. Florio had finished locking up for the night, but he opened the door for Emily and sold her a quart of milk. Then he pulled out a stool by the cash register and offered her a ginger cookie from his cookie jar. "What's wrong, my *bella* Emily?" he asked.

Emily settled herself on the stool and took a bite of the spicy cookie. Her spirits began to climb. Mr. Florio was always a good listener. "Well..." she began.

She was telling Mr. Florio her troubles when the store's doorbell jingled. Through the thin curtain on the glass front door, Emily could see two large men. Mr. Florio frowned. "Go upstairs, Emily," he said abruptly. "I have business to do."

Nobody wants me around, Emily thought bitterly as she left the store by the side exit. She was halfway upstairs before she realized her milk was still on the counter. *Dorothy's right,* she thought. *I would forget my head if it wasn't attached.*

She headed back down the steps. Her hand was on the doorknob when she heard a threatening voice. "Mr. M told us to give you a message, old man. If you don't pay up, something bad could happen." Emily heard cans falling. "It could happen real soon."

Stunned, Emily stood by the door, listening.

"Get out of my store," Mr. Florio ordered hoarsely. "Or I'll—"

She heard a crunching thud, a groan of pain, then a crash. Trembling, she opened the door a crack. Mr. Florio was lying facedown on the floor. Two men were standing over him. One man moved as if to kick Mr. Florio's motionless body.

"NO!" cried Emily. The two men turned toward her.

CHAPTER 2

WATCH OUT!

For a moment, both men stared at Emily. She stared back, frozen with fear. Then one of the thugs, a heavy man with a mole on his cheek, told the other, "Mr. M said there shouldn't be no witnesses."

The other man nodded. He had sharp features and eyes that darted like a suspicious ferret's. With a few long strides, he was across the store and looking down at Emily. She stood rigid, unable to move or speak.

Suddenly, a voice came from upstairs. "Emily!" Mother called.

"That your ma?" the ferret-faced man asked.

Emily tried to talk, but no words came out of her mouth. She heard Mother calling again, "Emileeeee! Dinner's almost ready."

"Answer me!" the man demanded. "That your ma calling you?"

"Yes," Emily answered, her voice barely a whisper.

"Let's get out of here," urged the thug who was standing over Mr. Florio.

The ferret-faced man nodded. He pointed a finger in Emily's face. "Watch out, kid. Don't say nothing to nobody, or you'll be sorry. Remember, we know where you live." He smiled a nasty smile. "And we know who you are, *Emily*."

The thugs strode out, banging the door behind them. As soon as they were gone, Emily rushed to Mr. Florio. "Are you all right?"

With a groan, the old man slowly sat up. Emily winced as she saw blood dripping from a gash on his forehead.

"I'll get my mother," she said breathlessly.

Mr. Florio grabbed her arm. "I fell. I will be all right."

"I saw what those men did to you. I'll go get help."

Mr. Florio looked confused. "You were here? You saw them? Did they see you?"

"Yes," Emily said. "But they've left. Let me go for help!"

"No!" Mr. Florio insisted. "Lock the door. Make sure they're gone."

Emily hurried to the front door and bolted it securely. Then she pulled aside the curtain and peered out onto Gardner Avenue. Her stomach lurched. The two thugs were standing right across the street!

As she watched, a long black Duesenberg motorcar, driven by a chauffeur, drew up. The car's windows were open, and a man in a business suit was sitting in the back. He had slicked-back dark hair, and he was smoking. As he brought his cigar to his mouth, Emily could see the glint of a diamond ring on his pinkie finger.

The thugs piled into the front seat, next to the driver. Emily saw them turn and talk to the cigar smoker, who sat alone in the back like a king on his throne. Whatever the thugs said seemed to anger him. He frowned and flicked his ashes into the street with a violent gesture.

Then he turned toward Florio's Foods. For a moment, he seemed to look straight at Emily. She had a brief image of a narrow face, deep-set dark eyes, and a thin mustache. Terrified, she dropped the curtain.

"Mr. Florio!" she whispered. "They're out there. They're looking over here!"

The old man struggled to his feet and staggered to the back of the store. He returned, grasping a rusty shotgun. Emily stared in disbelief. "You aren't going to use that, are you?"

"EMILEEEE!" Mother called again from upstairs.

"Go upstairs, Emily," Mr. Florio ordered. "This is no place for you."

Suddenly, tires squealed outside. Lifting a corner of the curtain, Emily looked out and saw the thugs' black car speeding away. Mr. Florio looked out, too. "They're gone," he said. "But I'll be ready for them next time."

He pulled out his handkerchief and wiped his forehead.

Emily saw the white handkerchief turn red with blood. "I'll be right back," she said.

She ran to the back of the store, where Mr. Florio kept a box of clean rags. She grabbed some cloths and hurried back to Mr. Florio.

"Who are those men?" she asked, handing him a clean square of cotton. "Why did they hit you?"

"They're gangsters," he said shortly. "Cheap criminals."

"Why did they come here? What do they want?"

"They make so much money selling liquor, they think they're big shots," Mr. Florio said bitterly. "They want everyone who does business around here to pay them pro-tection money—'insurance,' they call it. They say if we don't pay, they'll make sure we don't do business no more."

He shook his head sadly. "I came to America so I could live in a free country, and I've worked hard all my life. My only son died in the war, fighting for this country. Now these scum want me to pay for Mr. M's *protection.'*" He spat out the word. "Pah! I'll die before I pay them a dime."

Emily described the dark-haired man she'd seen in the backseat of the Duesenberg. "Is that Mr. M—the man they were talking about?"

Mr. Florio nodded. "Mr. M is an evil man, *cara*. He's boss of the gangsters around here, and he's got connec-tions in New York. People say he wants to be as big as Al Capone in Chicago." Mr. Florio looked at Emily with worried eyes. "Forget you ever heard Mr. M's name. And don't talk about what you saw. You'll be safer that way."

"What about you?" Emily asked. "Shouldn't we call the police?"

"It's no use. Some cops are all right, but there are too many who do whatever the gangsters pay them to do." Mr. Florio looked at his shotgun. "I'll handle this myself."

"But—" Emily started to protest.

Mother entered the store through the side door. "Emily, I've been calling and calling you! What's taking you so long?" she demanded. Then she saw Mr. Florio. She stopped short. "What happened?"

The old man smiled wryly. "I had visitors. They wanted to 'protect' me." He waved his hand at the fallen cans that littered the floor. "This is their idea of 'protection.'"

"You're hurt!" Mother exclaimed.

"No, no," said Mr. Florio. He touched his forehead. The bandage was already soaked with blood. "This is nothing. I'll be fine. But I wish your daughter had not been here. She saw what happened."

Mother looked at Emily, and the crease between her brows deepened. But when she spoke, her voice was surprisingly light. "Dinner is ready, Emily. You go upstairs. I'll stay and help Mr. Florio clean up."

"I can help, too," Emily offered. She began picking up cans of tomatoes.

"No, dear. Go upstairs now," Mother said firmly.

Reluctantly, Emily headed for the stairs. Once inside

the stairwell, she paused, straining to hear the conversation inside the store.

"It would have been better if that scum had not seen Emily," Mr. Florio was saying. "She should be careful. If you can, get her away from here for a while."

"Do you think they'll come back?" asked Mother.

Emily listened hard for Mr. Florio's reply, but she couldn't hear it. He and Mother must have moved too far from the door. Emily climbed slowly up the stairs, worry gripping her with every step. *If the gangsters do come back, will they be looking for me?*

As she walked upstairs, Dorothy ran down past her. "I'm going to the drugstore to telephone Bitsy," she said, her voice tight with anger. "Tell Mother I've gone."

Emily nodded. The corner drugstore was the only place with a public telephone that was open after six o'clock. Mother hoped to be able to afford a private telephone someday, but so far they did not have enough money.

When Emily opened the apartment door, she was met by the tempting odor of fried sausages and mashed potatoes. Usually, it was one of her favorite meals. Yet as she sat at the kitchen table, all she could think about was the ferret-faced man's warning, "Remember, we know where you live." And he knew her name was Emily. Would he come after her?

She pushed her plate of sausages away, and Homer looked at her pleadingly. "I wish you'd been there," Emily told him. "You would've bitten that man, wouldn't you?"

She fed the little dog crispy bits of sausage until she heard Mother's footsteps on the stairs. Then she whispered, "Go away. I can't give you any more." Homer seemed to understand. He retreated to his bed in the corner just as Mother walked in.

"I'm glad you started on dinner," Mother said. Her voice sounded cheerful, but her eyes looked worried.

Before Emily could ask what Mr. Florio had said, Dorothy rushed into the apartment. "Guess what!" she exclaimed. "I called Bitsy and told her I couldn't go to the beach with her because I had to stay with Emily. And you'll never guess what Bitsy said!"

"Well?" Mother asked.

"She said Emily could come along, too! The Brewsters have already reserved a double room just for me, so it wouldn't be any trouble or expense for them. And Bitsy says her mother *loves* children."

Dorothy just thinks of me as a child, Emily thought bitterly. *It's like we're not even sisters anymore.*

"Isn't that simply marvelous, Mother?" Dorothy asked. "Emily and I can both go!"

Emily waited for Mother to say that the whole idea was out of the question. But Mother seemed to consider the proposal seriously. After a few moments, she asked, "Would Mrs. Brewster be with you girls the whole time?"

Dorothy assured her that she would.

"Who else would be going?" Mother quizzed.

"No one," said Dorothy. "Of course, there'll be lots of guests at the resort. Bitsy says it's very well known. *All* the fashionable people go there!"

"You'd keep your sister with you, wouldn't you?" Mother probed. "You wouldn't go off with Bitsy and neglect Emily?"

"Of course not," Dorothy exclaimed. She looked shocked at the suggestion. "I'd watch Emily like a hawk!"

Finally, Mother turned to Emily. "Would you like to go, dear? Or would it be too difficult to be away from home?"

Emily considered the idea. It would be embarrassing to be dragged along on the trip, like an extra piece of baggage. How much nicer it would be if Dorothy really *wanted* her company. But she couldn't have Mother think she was scared to go away. And it would be wonderful to visit the beach . . .

"Yes, I'd like to go," Emily said finally.

"Perhaps that would be for the best," said Mother, half to herself. Then she nodded. "Very well, you may both go."

"Mother, you're the cat's pajamas!" Dorothy exclaimed. She gave Mother a big kiss on the cheek.

"I'm glad you think so," Mother said, smiling. "I hope you have a good time. It should be quite elegant."

Dorothy suddenly looked worried. "Of course, I'll *have* to have some new clothes—especially a new bathing suit. And I'll need at least one new evening dress—the Grand Atlantic is *very* formal."

"We don't have money for a new wardrobe, dear," Mother reminded her gently.

Dorothy thought for a moment, then jutted out her chin. Emily knew that look well. It meant Dorothy was determined to succeed—no matter what.

"That's all right, Mother," Dorothy said decisively. "I'll find material on sale and sew the clothes myself. I'll start looking for patterns tonight. But first I'd better call Bitsy. I can hardly wait to tell her I'm coming!" Dorothy raced out of the apartment. Emily could hear her running down the staircase.

Emily looked at Mother. "Shouldn't we tell Dorothy what happened—how those gangsters attacked Mr. Florio?"

"I'll tell her later," said Mother. "It's been a long time since I've seen Dorothy so happy. I don't want to spoil her joy so soon."

Then Mother looked very serious. "And remember, *you* mustn't tell *anyone* else what happened downstairs. Mr. Florio is quite insistent on that. He says it could put you in great danger. You understand, don't you?"

"Yes," said Emily, but she wondered what would happen if she did tell someone. *Would the gangsters come back to get me?*

"I'm glad you understand." Mother sighed and sat back in her chair. "I'm also glad you'll have the chance to get away for a bit. By the time you return, perhaps this trouble will have blown over."

Suddenly, Emily understood why Mother was allowing

the trip. *She thinks we'll be safer at the beach than here at home!*

Emily looked around their tidy kitchen with its starched white curtains on the window and the polished copper teakettle on the stove. Could she really be in danger in her own home?

Again, she remembered the words of the ferret-faced man. "Don't say nothing to nobody," he'd said. "Or you'll be sorry." She shuddered. The trip to the beach could not come soon enough.

CHAPTER 3

SMUGGLERS OF RUM ROW

For the next few days, Emily stayed inside as much as possible. Whenever she had to go outside, she worried that thugs would be out there, waiting to grab her as soon as she turned a corner.

Mr. Florio was watchful, too. He kept his shotgun near his cash register, and his brown eyes looked tired. "I'm glad you're leaving Monday," he told Emily. "You go enjoy yourself at the sea. And do not worry about anything."

She looked at Mr. Florio. One of his eyes had turned black and blue, and the gash on his forehead was purple. *How can I help but worry?* she wondered.

Monday finally arrived. As the sun rose over the city's smokestacks, Mother, Dorothy, and Emily traveled by trolley to Broad Street Station. The smell of exhaust and the rumble of trains filled the bustling station. Emily felt overwhelmed by the crowds. She wanted to reach for Mother's hand, but she stopped herself.

Mother mustn't know I'm scared, she thought. She put her free hand into her skirt pocket and walked behind Dorothy, who struggled under the weight of two suitcases.

Emily carried only one bag. She'd been careful to bring her sketching supplies: paper, charcoal pencils, and erasers. For clothes, she had packed just her "good" church dress (a hand-me-down from Dorothy), a sweater, two skirts, three blouses, a sailor suit for playing in the sand, and her old, scratchy bathing suit.

At least my suitcase is light, Emily thought as they hurried to catch the train to Shell Cove, New Jersey. When they reached the train platform, Mother gave them last-minute instructions. "Be careful in the ocean. And if you do get into trouble, don't panic. Stay calm and signal for help."

"Yes, yes, Mother, we know," said Dorothy impatiently. "We're good swimmers, and I'll keep an eye on Emily."

"Good," said Mother, smiling. "And, remember, mind your manners! And have a nice time!"

As the train pulled out, Emily's chest felt tight. She'd never left Mother before—and now she'd be gone for a whole week. Leaning out the train window, she called, "Good-bye, Mother! I'll draw pictures of everything and bring them home next week."

"Sit down!" Dorothy ordered in a low voice. "You're making a spectacle of yourself!"

The sisters sat across from each other on the train's wicker bench seats. Emily, who faced backward, saw

Philadelphia fade into the distance as the train crossed over the Delaware River. The train made its first stop in Camden, New Jersey, then began chugging toward the Jersey coast. Emily watched the scenery and the other passengers, while Dorothy became immersed in her book.

"What are you reading?" Emily asked.

Dorothy showed her the title: *Etiquette.* "It's written by Mrs. Emily Post," Dorothy explained. "It tells about manners and how things are done in the best society. For example, what would you think if I told you I was going to drive an auto and take some photos?"

"Hmmm," said Emily. "Well, first I'd wonder where you got the auto. Then I'd wonder if I could borrow your camera. I've always wanted to take a photo."

"No," said Dorothy, shaking her head. "You shouldn't use words like 'auto' and 'photo.' You should say 'automobile' and 'photograph.'"

"Does it really matter?"

"Your manners always matter if you want to belong in the best society," Dorothy lectured. "And you'd better watch your manners at the Grand Atlantic. I don't want you to embarrass me. You really should read this book."

"No, thanks," Emily said hastily. "I promised Mother I'd sketch the scenery."

Dorothy returned to *Etiquette.* Emily tried to draw the neat white farmhouses and acres of cornfields in the New Jersey countryside, but the scenes changed too fast, and the rumbling train jostled her pencil. Finally, she put away her sketching materials. Looking for something to do, she picked up a newspaper left on a nearby seat. A headline grabbed her attention: *AGENTS ARREST DANGEROUS GANG OF BOOTLEGGERS.*

A photo showed three federal agents leaning against crates of illegal liquor seized in a raid. Two of the men were short and heavy. The article didn't give their names, but Emily wondered if they might be Izzy Einstein and Moe Smith. Agents Einstein and Smith had become famous for their success in catching bootleggers, and they often used clever disguises to fool the criminals.

The third agent was taller and balding, with a large nose and a muscular build. While the two short men looked serious, the third man half smiled from under his handlebar mustache. He looked as though he couldn't quite hide his pride in the big arrest.

Emily studied the photo, then read how the agents had raided a huge bootlegging operation. They had seized illegal alcohol worth thousands of dollars and had rounded up five gang members. Some of the gang had been armed with machine guns and were considered extremely dangerous. The article ended with the words "See Editorial."

Turning to the editorial page, Emily found a column entitled "Threat to Civilization." The editor praised the arrests and said that gangsters were a growing threat. "Like modern-day Western outlaws, these gangsters take anything they want and kill anyone who gets in their way," he wrote.

Kill anyone who gets in their way! Emily thought. Her stomach gave a sickening twist.

According to the editorial, two of the men arrested had been caught once before. Their case had gone to trial, and a key witness had been willing to testify about their activities. But just before he was scheduled to testify, the witness had disappeared. He had never been seen again and was presumed dead. Without the witness's testimony, the gangsters had gone free.

"We hope and pray that, this time, justice will be served," the editorial concluded.

When Emily put down the paper, there were goose bumps all over her arms. She showed the newspaper to Dorothy. "Look," she whispered. "These gangsters have machine guns — and they killed a witness who was going to testify against them. What if the gangsters who attacked Mr. Florio come back with a machine gun? Or what if they come after me because *I'm* a witness?"

Dorothy looked up. Mother had given her a very brief account of the attack on Mr. Florio. Mr. Florio, however, had later insisted to Dorothy that the incident was "nothing to worry about." Dorothy had been inclined to believe him.

Now Dorothy glanced at her sister. "Don't be such a nervous Nellie! Those men you saw at Mr. Florio's store were just neighborhood toughs trying to bully an old man."

"They were gangsters!" Emily insisted. "Mr. Florio told me they were."

"Well, even if they were, you'll probably never see another gangster again," Dorothy said confidently. "So don't worry about it. Here's something you really should study."

While Emily had been reading the newspaper, her sister had borrowed her paper and charcoal pencil. Emily stared unbelievingly at Dorothy's sketch. It was a picture of an elaborate table setting, complete with several different knives, forks, and spoons. "I know how to use a knife and fork! Why should I study that?"

"I'll bet you don't know what this is," Dorothy said, pointing to a tiny fork.

"A fork for babies?" Emily guessed.

"No," said Dorothy triumphantly. "It's an oyster fork. You use it to dig oysters out of their shells."

"Ugh!" Emily made a face. "I don't even like oysters."

"If we're served them at the hotel, you must eat at least one to be polite. And you must use this fork." Dorothy patted the seat next to her. "Sit over here. I have lots of things to show you before we get to Shell Cove. You'll have to know how to behave properly."

For the rest of the train ride, Emily endured her sister's lectures on the differences between a fish fork and a salad fork, how to dine in an elegant restaurant, and how to make polite conversation.

At last the train pulled into the Shell Cove station.

The sky was bright blue, and the air smelled clean and salty. A young, dark-haired man in a chauffeur's uniform met them. He smiled and tipped his cap. "Miss Scott?"

Dorothy nodded, and he picked up the girls' suitcases. "The car is over here, miss," he said, pointing to a silver Rolls-Royce. "Miss Brewster asked me to bring you to the hotel. My name is Richards."

Richards opened the car door, and the sisters settled in the back of the luxurious motorcar. The smooth leather seats were a welcome relief from the train's wicker benches. "What a nice auto . . . automobile," Emily exclaimed.

Dorothy frowned at her, but the chauffeur laughed as he slid behind the wheel. "It *is* nice, isn't it, miss? A year ago there were more cars like this around here. Now it's one of the best in Shell Cove."

"Why were there more a year ago?" asked Emily, her curiosity getting the better of her shyness.

As he drove, the chauffeur explained that Shell Cove was in the midst of Rum Row, a section of coast stretching from Long Island, New York, to Atlantic City, New Jersey. It was called Rum Row because ships carrying rum—and other illegal liquor—sailed here from foreign countries. The ships' captains, called rumrunners, would anchor in international waters, just three miles offshore.

"On a clear day, you could see the rumrunners' ships from the beach," he recalled. "They lined up out there like cows in a barn waiting for milking. Anyone with a fast boat could speed out and buy a cargo of liquor, then come back and sell it at a profit. The bootleggers made a lot of money. And," Richards chuckled, "they bought some real nice cars."

Emily looked out the window at Shell Cove. The town's streets were lined with well-kept houses. An American flag fluttered above the library, and mothers with baby carriages promenaded along the sidewalks. *Is it possible that bootleggers could be here, too?* she wondered.

She found it easy to talk to the chauffeur. He didn't turn around and stare at her; he looked straight ahead, concentrating on steering the big motorcar. Emily asked, "What about the police? Couldn't they stop the bootleggers?"

The chauffeur explained that so many small boats had been involved in smuggling, it had been impossible for the Coast Guard to catch them all. But, he added, things had changed. Congress recently had moved the international waters limit to about twelve miles offshore—a challenging distance for any but the best boats. "Coast Guard patrols have cracked down on the rumrunners," Richards said. "Now it's quieter around here."

"So there's no more Rum Row?" Emily asked hopefully. "No more smuggling?"

"Some rumrunners still come," Richards admitted. "They say gangsters from New York and Philly are willing to pay big money for foreign liquor." The chauffeur shook his head. "But you'd have to be crazy—or have a real good boat—to take the risks."

Emily wanted to ask more questions, but her sister shot her a disapproving glance. "Are we almost there, Richards?" Dorothy asked in her I-am-the-boss tone. "I see a sign ahead."

"Yes, miss," said Richards, again sounding formal. "Here we are." He turned the Rolls-Royce onto a curving, pebbled driveway. A two-story brick building stood just beyond an iron gate. A sign announced "Grand Atlantic Hotel." Emily felt disappointed. The brick building was hardly larger than a Philadelphia townhouse.

"Is this what they call a 'grand' hotel?" Emily whispered.

Dorothy looked confused. "I guess so," she whispered back. "Maybe it has a nice view of the ocean."

As the car idled in front of the gate, a stout man in a red uniform stepped out of the building. "May I help you?"

"Miss Dorothy Scott and Miss Emily Scott," Richards replied. "They're guests of Miss Brewster."

The stout man nodded, and another man in a red uniform opened the gate. The chauffeur drove through. But instead of stopping in front of the brick building, the Rolls-Royce continued down the driveway.

Then they turned a corner. Ahead stood a magnificent white building. It stretched longer than a city block and stood four stories high. At each of the roof's corners, a turret rose into the sky, giving the structure a castlelike air.

"Zowie!" breathed Emily.

CHAPTER 4

A SURPRISE ENCOUNTER

The chauffeur smiled. "Welcome to the Grand Atlantic!"

Emily gazed at the elegant hotel and felt a glow of relief. *Surely,* she thought, *we'll be safe here!* A red-uniformed door-man ushered them into the lobby. Emily glanced around. Thick red Oriental rugs carpeted the floor, and red velvet cur-tains draped the windows. The white vaulted ceiling was trimmed with gold, and an enormous chandelier glistened from the ceiling.

Emily felt small and shabby amid the grandeur. "I guess that other building wasn't the hotel after all," she whispered.

"Of course not," Dorothy whispered back, as if she had known it all along. "That was just the gatehouse."

With an air of confidence, Dorothy led the way to the main desk. Richards followed with the suitcases. "I'm Miss Scott," Dorothy began. "And I'm—"

"Dodo, darling!" a high voice called out.

Dodo! thought Emily. *What kind of a name is that?* She turned and saw a petite girl in a bright blue dress hurrying across the lobby. The girl had bobbed blonde hair and a bow-shaped mouth outlined in red lipstick. A silver cigarette holder dangled from her hand.

"You're here at last!" the girl exclaimed, hugging Dorothy. "Just in time!"

"Bitsy! It's so good to see you!" exclaimed Dorothy. "You look marvelous!" The two girls chattered excitedly for a few minutes. Then Dorothy remembered Emily. "Bitsy, this is my sister," she said, introducing her. "Emily, this is Bitsy Brewster."

"How do you do?" Emily said, recalling her sister's careful instructions.

Bitsy giggled. "Oh, Dodo, she's so sweet! We're going to have so much fun!"

Emily's cheeks grew hot. *I did just what Dorothy told me to,* she thought. *And her friend laughs at me as if I'm a trained monkey.* She shot her sister an accusing look, but Dorothy had linked arms with Bitsy and the two girls were walking away together.

"Don't worry about signing in, Dodo, darling," Bitsy assured her. "We've done all that for you. Richards will send up your bags. You come with me. I have some very exciting news!"

Emily followed Bitsy and Dorothy across the elegant

entrance hall. A sweeping staircase graced the center of
the lobby. Near the staircase stood an immense grand
piano. A man in a tuxedo was playing a Mozart sonata.
Music echoed through the lobby.

"What a marvelous piano!" Dorothy exclaimed. "And
he plays beautifully."

"I've heard you play, and you're twice as good," said
Bitsy. "Sometime you should pound out tunes down here."

"Oh, I couldn't," said Dorothy, but she looked yearn-
ingly toward the piano as they passed.

Three elevators stood beyond the stairs. Bitsy entered
the closest one. It was paneled in highly polished wood,
and a brass rail stood at waist height.

"Third floor," Bitsy told the operator, a thin, glum man
who sat on a tall stool by the elevator's controls.

"Yes, miss," said the man. He leaned from his stool and
pressed a shiny brass lever. As the elevator rose, Bitsy said,
"Dodo, you'll never guess who's coming to see us here!"

Emily looked at her sister in surprise. Dorothy had told
Mother that only the Brewsters would be at the hotel. Had
she been fibbing? But Dorothy looked mystified. "Someone
I know?"

"Ab-so-*lute*-ly!" exclaimed Bitsy.

"Who?"

"Oh, nobody special," Bitsy teased. "Only Chadwick
Wellingsford and Frank Preston!" She smiled triumphantly.
"They sailed here from New York. They're staying with

Chadwick's grandparents, who have a cottage nearby. And they're dining with us at the hotel tonight!"

Dorothy looked shocked. "Chadwick and Frank—here in Shell Cove? What a coincidence!"

"Actually, it's not really a coincidence," Bitsy said, lowering her voice. "Chadwick wrote me that he and Frank would be visiting Shell Cove, so I convinced Mummy that we should visit here, too. I told her you should come, so you and Frank and Chadwick and I could all spend time together." Bitsy beamed. "Wasn't that clever of me?"

"Why didn't you tell me before?" Dorothy demanded.

Bitsy lowered her voice even more. It was now barely a whisper, but Emily, who was standing just a foot away, overheard. "You said your mother was rather strict. I thought she might not let you come if she knew boys would be visiting."

Mother never would've allowed us to come! Emily thought.

"I *suppose* it'll be fine," Dorothy said doubtfully. "Still, I wish I'd known..."

Bitsy shrugged away her friend's concerns. "Well, now you're here, and the four of us will have a whole week together. Isn't that just the bee's knees?"

"Third floor," the elevator operator announced.

The girls stepped off into a mirrored foyer. Bitsy led them to the right, down a corridor where cream-colored walls were hung with pictures of the sea. Brass doorknobs shone on a long line of doors, and everything was spotless.

A uniformed bellboy had opened the door to 321, and he stood beside it with the girls' suitcases.

"I hope you like your rooms," Bitsy said as she swept by the bellboy. "Mummy and I have our rooms on the second floor, but they didn't have any more rooms on that floor. Mummy *insists* on second-floor suites. She didn't think you'd mind the third floor, though."

"I'm sure this will be fine," said Dorothy. The bellboy put down their bags, and Dorothy tipped him. Then she looked around the room. "It's beautiful!" she exclaimed. "And what a wonderful view!"

Emily stepped inside. For a moment, she was speechless. It was the prettiest room she'd ever seen. There was rose-patterned wallpaper on the walls, matching rose-colored chintz covered an armchair, and a vase of fresh roses stood on the dressing table. On a mahogany bureau sat a polished mirror and a shiny black telephone. To the right of the door was a four-poster bed. It had a lacy white cover and lots of plump pillows.

Across from the door, French windows opened onto a small balcony. The windows showed the wide, sandy beach in front of the hotel and the ocean beyond.

"We reserved two rooms for you since we didn't know if you'd be bringing your maid," Bitsy said offhandedly.

Dorothy and Emily shared a quick glance. *This is a different world!* Emily thought.

Bitsy opened a door on the right, which Emily had

assumed was a closet. "Each room has a bathroom," Bitsy said, walking into a gleaming, white-tiled, modern bath. Then she opened a door on the left wall. "And here's your other room. The two rooms connect, so you can keep the door open if you want."

The girls entered a second room, a twin of the first. The only difference was that this room had a lilac theme. Lilacs bloomed on the wallpaper and in the vase, and the armchair was covered in lilac-colored chintz. "We have two rooms!" Emily whispered to her sister. "And two bathrooms!"

"Shhh!" Dorothy whispered back. Aloud, she said, "This will be perfect, Bitsy."

"Good," said Bitsy. "If you need your gowns pressed for dinner, just give them to my maid, Clarice. She's quite good with an iron."

Bitsy whispered to Dorothy. Dorothy nodded and said, "Emily, Bitsy and I are going to her room. Why don't you unpack? We'll be back soon."

"Then we'll all take a stroll on the boardwalk," Bitsy added. "I'm simply dying to show you the beach."

"Where should I unpack?" Emily asked. "Which room?"

Dorothy shrugged. "Either one. It doesn't matter."

Emily heard her sister and Bitsy giggle as they walked down the corridor. Left alone, Emily looked again at the rose room, then the lilac. She could hardly believe her luck. Except when Dorothy had been away at college, they had always shared a bedroom. Now she was to have a room all to herself—with a bathroom and a balcony!

But which room? She paced between them and finally decided on the rose room. It reminded her of the garden they'd had in the country. She pulled Dorothy's heavy suitcases into the lilac room, then unpacked her own things in the rose room. She hung her clothes behind the louvered doors of the closet and folded her underwear in the sachet-scented bureau drawers. Finally, she arranged her sketching materials on the dressing table along with her comb and brush.

When she was finished, Emily sat back on the soft bed and sighed with satisfaction. *I wish I could live like this all the time!* she thought.

For a few minutes, she soaked up the luxury of the beautiful room. Then she glanced at the clock on the dresser. It was quarter past four. Dorothy and Bitsy had been gone quite a while. Surely, they wouldn't mind if she explored a bit . . .

The bellboy had left two iron keys on the dresser, one to the rose room, 321, and one to the lilac room, 323. Emily took the 321 key and ventured down the corridor. Along the way, she examined the ocean scenes on the walls. She especially liked a reproduction of a Winslow Homer painting. It showed a fisherman rowing a small boat on an angry sea. Looking at the picture, she could almost feel the wind in her hair. *Someday,* she thought, *I'll be able to paint like that.*

Emily walked past the elevators and stopped at the winding staircase that led down to the main floor. Looking over the railing, she saw people strolling in the lobby below. She leaned out a little farther and was startled by a familiar-sounding *woof!*

She looked down. On the landing just beneath her, a small sausage-shaped dog was tied by its leash to the wrought-iron railing. The little dog wagged its tail and looked up at Emily expectantly. She hurried down the stairs and knelt beside it.

"Hello!" she said, stroking its long, silky brown fur. "What's your name? And what are you doing here?"

"That's Max," a girl's voice replied. "He's waiting for me."

Turning, Emily saw a slim girl with bright red hair making her way down the hall. Her legs were encased in heavy braces, but she moved quickly, swinging herself on crutches.

"I'm sorry," said Emily, feeling embarrassed. She stood up, trying not to stare at the girl's braces. She knew the other girl probably had suffered from polio, a sickness that struck suddenly, often with a high fever. Polio killed some victims and left many others with weak or paralyzed limbs. "I didn't mean to bother your dog," Emily apologized.

The girl laughed cheerfully. "Look at him—he's not bothered! He's happy to meet you."

It was true. Max was jumping, trying to reach up and lick Emily's hand. Emily smiled at the dog's enthusiasm and started petting him. "I have a dachshund at home, but he's bigger and he's got short hair." She scratched behind Max's ear. "Max is awfully cute, though."

"Thanks," said the girl. "He's one of my favorites." She put out her hand. "By the way, I'm Gwen Chapman. Do you like dogs?"

Emily shook the girl's hand and introduced herself. She usually had trouble talking to strangers, but this girl was about her own age, and she was so friendly that Emily soon found herself caught up in conversation. She told Gwen about Homer and how she missed him already, even though she'd been away from home less than a day.

"You're lucky to have your dog here with you," Emily said, a little enviously.

Gwen explained that Max wasn't her dog; he belonged to guests. "My uncle manages the hotel, and my mum is a telephone operator here. In the summers, I come to work with Mum, so I started my own business here taking care of guests' pets. Guests can spend the day swimming or golfing and still know their pets will be all right."

"Do many guests bring pets?"

"Oh, yes," said Gwen. "Little ones only, though. We don't accept big animals." She unfastened Max's leash from the railing and slipped it onto her wrist, just above where she held her crutch. "This week I'm taking care of one parrot, a Siamese cat, and a poodle—and Max. I just took the poodle back to her room. Now I'm taking Max back to his."

Emily was amazed. This girl was crippled, but she seemed so confident and businesslike. "Do you like doing it—taking care of pets, I mean?"

"Geez! I wouldn't do it unless I liked it!" Gwen exclaimed. "I love pets. I have three guinea pigs at home. I'd have more animals, but Mum says we don't have room."

"That's what my mother tells me!" said Emily. Gwen started walking Max down the corridor, and Emily fell into step beside her. She had just begun to tell Gwen about the animals she'd had to leave behind on the farm when she heard Dorothy calling "Emily!"

Emily turned and saw Dorothy walking toward her. "Where have you been?" Dorothy demanded. "I tried to get into our rooms. They were locked, and you were nowhere to be found. I wish you wouldn't wander off!"

Why does Dorothy always talk to me as if I'm five years old? Emily thought. "I was only looking around a bit," she defended herself, and she introduced Gwen.

Dorothy said hello, then turned to Emily impatiently. "We need to meet Bitsy downstairs. Come on!"

"Good-bye," Gwen said, smiling at Emily. "Maybe I'll see you later."

"Maybe," Emily agreed, wishing they'd had more time to talk. "Good-bye."

☙

Emily walked behind Dorothy and Bitsy as they headed toward the ocean. The afternoon was hot, and the sun glistened off the blue-green sea. Emily yearned to walk on the beach and dive into the waves. She asked if they could go swimming.

Bitsy laughed. "Heavens, no! We have to dress for dinner tonight. We wouldn't want to ruin our hair!"

"We'll go swimming another day," Dorothy said. "This afternoon we'll explore the boardwalk."

They followed the hotel's path across the sand dunes until they came to Shell Cove's busy boardwalk, which stretched down the beach, parallel to the sea. On this beautiful June day, the boardwalk was filled with couples walking arm in arm and sunburned children carrying sand pails and shovels.

Along the western side of the boardwalk, Emily saw a sign for Davis's Dressing Rooms, which advertised "Clean and Comfortable Accommodations for Changing Bathing Attire." There were food stands, too, with tempting smells of hot dogs and saltwater taffy. Emily heard organ music being played inside a covered pavilion. "Oh, it's a carousel!" she called out excitedly. "Can we take a ride?"

"Perhaps later," said Dorothy. She and Bitsy continued past the carousel, but Emily stopped to watch the prancing wooden horses. One tall white horse had a golden saddle. It shone in the afternoon sun, and Emily looked at it longingly.

After a few minutes, she looked up and discovered that Dorothy and Bitsy were now far ahead. Emily hurried to catch up, weaving her way among the vacationers. A rainbow of colorful clothes swept by her—girls in bright cotton dresses, men in straw hats. *No one looks drab and gray like they do in the city,* Emily thought happily.

Just then a man in a dark business suit caught her eye. As he passed by about ten feet away, she glanced up curiously at his face. Suddenly, she felt as if she'd been punched in the stomach.

The man was Mr. M.

CHAPTER 5

DANGER AT THE DANCE

For a moment Emily stood still, the crowd swirling past her. Then, heart pounding, she raced down the boardwalk. When she finally reached Dorothy and Bitsy, she pulled her sister aside.

"Mr. M is here!" Emily gasped. "I just saw him on the boardwalk."

"Where?" Dorothy looked around.

"He's gone now—he was walking the other way," said Emily, her voice rising. "He passed right by me!"

"Calm down!" said Dorothy. "How can you be so sure it's him?"

"I saw him when Mr. Florio was attacked. Mr. M was in his car across the street. For a moment he looked right at me!"

"For a moment?" Dorothy echoed. Her voice was full of skepticism. "You saw this man, Mr. M, for a moment— across the street and in a car. And now you say you recognize him again, here in Shell Cove?"

"Yes! I recognize his face—*and* his hair. It's dark and slicked back. And he's wearing the same kind of suit he wore that day," Emily insisted. "Don't you believe me?"

Dorothy glanced at Bitsy, who was waiting a few yards away. Then she turned back to her sister. "I'm sure you *think* you saw him again, Em. But thousands of dark-haired men wear business suits. Can you swear that the man you saw is the same man who was on our street last week?"

Emily hesitated. "I couldn't *swear* it was Mr. M," she admitted. "But he looked just like him."

"He probably did," Dorothy said reassuringly. "And if you see him again, point him out to me. In the meantime, forget about gangsters." She gestured at the beach. "We're on vacation. Let's enjoy ourselves."

Emily looked around the sunny boardwalk. Maybe Dorothy was right. Maybe she'd mistaken an innocent businessman for Mr. M. "All right," she agreed. "I'll try."

"Good girl!" said Dorothy. She took Emily's arm and steered her back toward Bitsy.

"Everything all right?" Bitsy asked. Dorothy nodded, and Emily tried to muster a smile. Yet she couldn't silence her fear. If that *was* Mr. M, what was he doing here?

By the time they returned to the hotel, it was past six. Emily's stomach had begun to growl, but Dorothy informed her that dinner would not be till eight.

"Eight o'clock!" Emily protested. "Can't we eat earlier?"

"We'll be dining with everyone else, and that's when fashionable people eat," Dorothy said firmly. "Wear your best dress. And, for goodness' sake, fix your hair!"

Emily took a bath, put on her Sunday dress, and braided her hair into two neat pigtails. Then she went to Dorothy's room. She was surprised to find her sister sitting at the dressing table, carefully applying rouge to her face.

"You needn't tell Mother I use rouge," Dorothy said, not turning away from her mirror. "She might not approve."

Emily nodded. "Mother says makeup is for fast girls— girls who smoke and drink. She says girls look prettier when they don't use any makeup."

"Mother may say that, but lots of pretty girls at college use makeup—and they don't all smoke or drink," said Dorothy. She outlined her mouth in red lipstick, then smiled into the mirror. She looked so grown-up that, to Emily, she almost seemed a stranger.

Emily gathered her courage. "Do you?" she asked.

"Do I what?"

"Do you smoke and drink? I know Bitsy smokes—I saw her cigarette holder."

"I tried smoking," Dorothy admitted. "But cigarettes made me sick. Besides, smoking makes your teeth yellow." She smiled again at the mirror, and her white teeth gleamed.

"What about drinking?"

"I tried that once, too. Someone gave me a drink at a party." Dorothy's mouth puckered. "Ugh! It tasted like tar! And then I heard a terrible story . . ." She paused.

"What?"

"Well," Dorothy confided, "there was a janitor who worked in our dormitory. He was a nice man—everybody liked him. One day we heard he was in the hospital. It turns out he'd drunk some bootleg whiskey, and it must have been made wrong. He ended up blinded for life." Dorothy shuddered. "Ever since then, I've stuck to soda pop."

Emily felt relieved. But she had one more question. "Why do you let Bitsy call you Dodo? It's such a silly name. And you told *me* you wanted to be called Dorothy."

Dorothy applied another coat of lipstick, then turned to face her. Emily had to admit that her sister looked beautiful—even with makeup.

"I don't really like it, but all the popular girls at college have nicknames, and that's mine. Bitsy would think I was a real wet blanket if I told her to stop calling me that." Dorothy shrugged. "So, I guess I'll live with it. Now help me button my dress, will you?" She handed Emily the peacock-blue evening gown she had just finished sewing the night before. "It's time to go downstairs."

They walked into the dining room at exactly eight o'clock. The elegant room was bright with candlelight, and a string quartet was playing softly. The tables were filled with men wearing black dinner jackets and ladies wearing diamonds and evening gowns.

The maître d' showed the girls to the Brewsters' table. Bitsy, who looked radiant in a yellow silk dress, introduced them to her mother, a chubby woman who wore a heavy diamond pendant with matching diamond earrings.

Emily hated meeting new people, especially grown-ups, but she remembered Dorothy's instructions. She curtsied. "How do you do, Mrs. Brewster?"

"How do you do?" Mrs. Brewster answered with a nod and an artificial smile. As soon as they were seated, she turned her attention to Dorothy. "Bitsy has told me *so* much about you, but she didn't mention where your family's from. Are you by chance related to Judge and Mrs. Erwin Scott from New Haven?"

Dorothy told her politely that her family was from Philadelphia and they had no relatives in New Haven, Connecticut.

"No? What a pity," said Mrs. Brewster. Her mouth was still smiling, but her eyes surveyed Dorothy critically. "Where exactly in Philadelphia is your family's home?"

Emily watched her sister hesitate. *Dorothy is ashamed of us,* she realized.

"We live near Miss Andrews' Academy," Dorothy said, smoothly mentioning the well-known school. "I was a student at Miss Andrews'. My sister goes there now."

"Really?" Mrs. Brewster replied. "And—"

"Oh, look, here come Chadwick and Frank!" Bitsy said, interrupting her mother. "Yoo-hoo, boys!"

Two tall, blond young men, both in tuxedos, arrived at the Brewsters' table. The first boy was very thin. He had an upturned nose and carefully slicked-back hair. Bitsy introduced him as Chadwick Wellingsford.

"Chadwick!" Mrs. Brewster welcomed the boy warmly. "So nice to meet you! Come sit by me!"

Bitsy introduced the second boy. "Mother, I'd like you to meet Frank Preston, Chadwick's friend from Columbia University. Frank is quite a football star!" Frank smiled modestly. His hair was not as neat as Chadwick's, but he had the strong build of an athlete and his smile showed deep dimples. He took a seat next to Dorothy.

As soon as the boys were seated, waiters brought the first course, a creamy chicken soup. There was a confusing array of silverware on the table, but Emily picked what she thought was the soupspoon. She looked across the table at her sister and saw Dorothy nod ever so slightly.

Phew! thought Emily. *I guessed right!*

For Emily, the rest of the meal was like an etiquette exam. Every time a new course arrived, she searched her place setting for the correct silverware. When the fish course arrived, she found her fish fork. For the main course, roast lamb with parsleyed potatoes, Emily opted for her largest knife and fork. Next the waiters served a salad, and Emily chose what she thought had to be her salad fork.

She was getting awfully full, but she munched a few bites of lettuce just to be polite.

No wonder Mrs. Brewster is chubby, she thought. *I would be too if I ate this much food every night.*

Finally the waiters brought dessert: a scoop of strawberry ice cream topped with whipped cream and a single strawberry. Emily discovered she still had some appetite left. She savored the sweet pink ice cream and listened to Chadwick tell about the boys' trip from New York City.

"We had a simply swell time in the city," Chadwick said, his Adam's apple bobbing enthusiastically. "Swanky parties every night, red-hot nightclubs—the whole nine yards. But we decided it was simply time to shove off for a while. So I took out my yacht, *Lady Luck,* and we headed down here. Great time we had on the high seas, eh, Frank?"

Frank looked up from his conversation with Dorothy. "Great!" he agreed. "I grew up boating on Lake Erie, but this was my first time on the Atlantic. *Lady Luck* cruised like a charm."

Chadwick beamed. "*Lady Luck*'s new—Father bought her for my birthday, and she's simply the bee's knees. Fastest little yacht I've ever had."

"I bet she's beautiful," sighed Bitsy. "Could we see her?"

"Of course!" Chadwick laughed. "Say, why don't we take her out for a spin tomorrow? We can all go!"

"I'm no sailor, but you young people should go," said Mrs. Brewster, beaming. "You'll have a wonderful time!"

It was decided that Chadwick and Frank would take the girls out on the boat the next morning. *I'd rather go swimming,* Emily thought. No one asked her opinion, though, so she nibbled her ice cream and said nothing.

After dinner, Mrs. Brewster excused herself to play bridge. Chadwick and Frank suggested that the girls go with them to the hotel ballroom. "The orchestra here is the cat's pajamas," Chadwick declared. "Let's cut a rug!"

"What does he mean?" Emily whispered to her sister.

"He wants to go dancing," Dorothy translated.

Emily followed Dorothy and her friends to the ballroom at the opposite end of the lobby. As they approached, they could hear an orchestra playing a waltz. "They play the old fogies' music first. Later they'll play the good stuff," Chadwick told his friends as they walked in.

An immense crystal chandelier hung over the center of the ballroom, reflecting light from the vaulted, gold-trimmed ceiling. Dozens of couples were waltzing on the polished floor. Around the sides of the ballroom, men and women in evening dress watched the dancers and sipped punch from long-stemmed glasses.

Bitsy, Chadwick, Dorothy, and Frank soon joined the waltzing couples. Emily stood among the spectators and watched. She decided that Bitsy and Chadwick looked nice enough together—both were blond and both were fairly good dancers. But Dorothy and Frank made a truly striking pair. Dorothy was dark and slim, while Frank was blond and muscular. Both were superb dancers.

Listening to the music, Emily wished that she, too, could whirl around the dance floor. Dorothy must have read her mind, because she whispered something to Frank. He escorted Dorothy to a table and then walked over to Emily. "Would you care to dance?" he asked, smiling.

Emily took a deep breath and nodded. Trying hard to recall the dancing lessons she'd had at school, she accompanied Frank onto the floor. Although she stepped on his foot once, he smiled and made easy conversation, asking how she liked the hotel and whether she enjoyed the beach.

Emily began to relax. *This is fun,* she thought as she glided across the floor. *And it's not nearly as hard as it looks.*

When the music ended, Emily glanced up at Frank to thank him for the dance. She was startled to see a look of shock on his face. For a moment, she thought she'd done something terribly wrong. Then she realized that he was staring over her head.

She turned and saw a dark-haired man in a black tuxedo standing among the crowd of onlookers. The man nodded slightly at Frank, then walked away. Emily felt fear like a chunk of ice in her stomach. "Wh-who is that you were looking at?" she asked Frank, her voice shaking.

Frank seemed to pull himself away from his thoughts. He shook his head. "No one," he said. "No one at all."

CHAPTER 6

A CRY FOR HELP

As Frank escorted her off the dance floor, Emily scanned the ballroom. Although she'd seen him for only a second, the man who had nodded to Frank had looked disturbingly like Mr. M. But the ballroom was filled with people, and almost all the men were wearing tuxedos. Emily did not see the dark-haired man anywhere.

I must have been imagining it, she told herself.

When she and Frank reached Dorothy's table, Frank offered to get punch for both girls. "No, thank you," said Emily, who felt suddenly tired from the long day. She turned to Dorothy and asked in a low voice, "Can we go upstairs soon?"

Dorothy opened her purse and handed her the key to 321. "You go ahead."

"By myself? Aren't you coming?"

"Honestly, I don't think you need an escort to take

an elevator to the third floor," Dorothy said. "You can find your way to the room, can't you?"

"Well, yes," said Emily. "But I thought . . ."

"You'll be perfectly safe," Dorothy assured her. "After all, this is one of the finest hotels in the country." She rose from the table and took Frank's arm. "We'll just have a few more dances. I'll be up to the room by midnight."

Emily watched her sister and Frank return to the dance floor. *Dorothy doesn't want to be with me at all,* she thought. *She wishes I'd just go away.*

Holding tightly to her key, Emily left the ballroom. As she crossed the wide lobby, she couldn't help checking to see if the dark-haired man was anywhere in sight. She saw dowagers with heavy strings of pearls, bald men in too-tight tuxedos, and well-dressed couples strolling arm in arm. But no one looked remotely like Mr. M.

Emily tried to shake off her fears. *A gangster would never be here,* she told herself firmly. *Not at one of the finest hotels in the country.*

She stood near the waiting elevators, but she couldn't quite bring herself to go upstairs alone. As she wondered what to do, she heard laughter coming from the east wing. She remembered the list of "Evening Entertainments" she'd seen posted by the front desk. She hesitated, tempted to go exploring but wondering whether she should. Finally, she decided that Dorothy didn't care where she went—and almost anything would be better than sitting alone upstairs.

Cautiously, Emily ventured into the well-lit corridor that led to the east wing. In the elegant Princeton Room, she saw about two dozen bridge players sitting at small square tables. Guests clustered in chairs around the edge of the room, watching the games. Emily thought she'd join the onlookers, but then she spotted Mrs. Brewster among the bridge players. *If Mrs. Brewster sees me,* Emily thought, *she'll probably send me straight upstairs.*

Emily decided to keep exploring. She discovered that the next room, the Harvard Room, was decorated with Chinese hanging lanterns and filled with people playing mah-jongg. Players in Chinese robes were arguing and laughing as they clacked their mah-jongg tiles. Emily had read about mah-jongg in magazines, but she'd never seen it played. She would have liked to stay and watch the game, but she felt out of place among all the costumed adults. She continued down the hall.

The last room along the corridor, the Yale Room, was so dark that at first Emily couldn't see inside it. She joined a small crowd standing just inside the entrance. When her eyes adjusted to the dim light, she saw several people sitting at a large table in the middle of the room. They all had their eyes closed, and they looked serious. A thin, very pale middle-aged woman sat at the head of the table. She was wearing a dark purple gown with a matching turban, and she was reaching out with her hands to some invisible presence.

"Speak to us, spirits! Speak to your beloved ones!" the woman called out in a high voice.

Emily realized she was watching a séance, and a chill ran down her back. She knew many people believed that they could communicate with dead loved ones through séances. The leader, called the medium, was supposed to have special powers. *But people can't really talk to the dead,* Emily thought. *Can they?*

Emily felt goose bumps on her arms as she watched the woman in purple fall into a trance. The woman rocked slowly, her eyes closed and her arms stretched out in front of her. "Come to us, spirits. Come to us!"

A whisper came from behind Emily. "Any minute now, Madame Serena is going to start shaking. She always does."

Emily spun around and saw Gwen. The redheaded girl was sitting in a wheelchair, which she had wheeled inside the door.

"Hello!" Emily whispered. "Why are you still here? Don't you have to go home?"

"Mum's working late tonight," Gwen whispered back. "My brother George is coming to pick me up. While I wait, I thought I'd watch Madame Serena. She's always—"

"HUSH!" an imperious voice ordered. Madame Serena opened her eyes and pointed at the two girls. "Begone! The spirits must have complete silence!"

"Let's go," muttered Gwen. She wheeled out the door, and Emily followed.

"I should go wait outside—that's where George picks me up," Gwen said. "Want to come with me?"

Emily hesitated. Dorothy was probably still dancing. And after the séance, Emily felt more spooked than ever. It would be nice to have someone to talk to. "All right," she agreed. "I guess I can go for a few minutes."

The girls went back to the lobby, but instead of turning toward the main door, Gwen headed for the dining room. "Where are you going?" Emily asked.

"To the kitchen entrance. This way."

Emily followed her down a corridor behind the dining room. They passed the kitchens and came to an exit, where two men in white uniforms were pushing carts filled with sacks of potatoes. "Evenin', Gwen," one of the men said, holding the door for her. "I haven't seen your brother yet."

"Thanks, Charlie," said Gwen, wheeling through the door. "It's a nice night. We'll wait outside."

There was a ramp outside the door, and Gwen rolled her chair down it. "I love this ramp," she said with a laugh. "They built it for the food carts, but it makes the door easy for me, too. I like it so much that George is building one for our front door at home. It'll be the berries!"

Emily joined Gwen outside. There was a full moon, and the cool evening air smelled like the sea. The kitchen entrance wasn't nearly as glamorous as the guest entrances, but the grounds were tidy. There was a circular driveway where trucks could pull up and unload food. Near the

driveway were several benches. Gwen pulled her wheelchair up to a bench, and Emily took a seat beside her.

"Do you think Madame Serena really talks to spirits?"
she asked Gwen.

"I don't know," Gwen admitted. "She's been here a few
weeks, and I've watched her a bunch of times. Sometimes
I think she's making it all up. Other times, it seems she
knows things she couldn't possibly find out without talking to a spirit."

"Really?" asked Emily. "Like what?"

"Well, once she asked if a woman named Rita was in
the audience. A lady stood up and said her name was Rita.
Madame Serena said she had a message from Archie. The
lady got very excited and said her brother Archie had died
in the war. Madame Serena said Archie wanted her to know
that he was at peace and that Rita shouldn't worry anymore.
The lady fainted, and her husband had to carry her out."

Emily felt goose bumps again. "Do many soldiers who
died send messages to their families?" she asked.

"Lots of people come to the séances because they want
to talk to husbands or brothers or sons who died." Gwen
paused. "I know how they feel," she added, her voice
suddenly serious. "My dad died in the war. I'd give a lot
to be able to talk to him."

"My father died in the war, too," Emily told her friend.
"Do you think I could talk to him through Madame
Serena?"

Gwen shook her head. "My mum says no. She says there's no such thing as ghosts. But sometimes I wonder. I know people who swear they've seen a ghost right here at the hotel. Her name's Bridget."

Emily looked around the deserted driveway. Despite the moon, the night suddenly seemed darker than before. "What happened to her?"

"There was an outbreak of typhus fever," Gwen explained. "Bridget was a chambermaid here, and she got really sick. Another maid named Annie was supposed to take care of her, but Annie was scared she'd get typhus, too. Instead of nursing Bridget, Annie just left trays of food outside Bridget's room. Bridget was too weak to go get the trays, so she had nothing to eat or drink. She died in her room, all alone."

"How terrible!" Emily exclaimed.

"What happened later was even worse," Gwen continued. "Soon after Bridget died, Annie ran down the hall one night, screaming. She swore she'd seen Bridget's ghost. Annie quit the hotel that night and never came back."

"Where was the ghost?" Emily asked breathlessly.

"Up in Bridget's room," Gwen said. She pointed to the top of the hotel. "On the fourth floor, near the north end. To this day, no one will sleep in that room, so they use it for storage."

"Oh," said Emily, a little weakly. Her room was on the third floor, near the north end of the hotel. She wanted to ask more about the ghost, but an old truck rattled up.

"Hey, Shrimp!" a friendly voice called. A smiling young man, trim and handsome in his Coast Guard uniform, hopped out of the truck. Gwen introduced Emily to her brother, George.

"Any friend of Shrimp's is a friend of mine," he said, shaking hands with Emily.

"My name's not Shrimp!" Gwen said with mock anger.

"I don't know," George teased. "You're small and red. You look like a shrimp to me." He ruffled his sister's red hair. "Come on, Shrimp, time to go home." George scooped up Gwen and settled her in the front seat of his truck. Then he put her wheelchair in the back.

"Bye!" Gwen called as they drove away. "Don't worry about Bridget—no one's seen her in ages."

"Bye," said Emily. "I won't worry." She tried to sound casual, but her pulse was racing as she hurried back inside the hotel and down the deserted kitchen corridor. She kept looking over her shoulder to make sure no one, alive or dead, was following her.

Finally, she reached the busy lobby. She glanced at the grandfather clock near the entry; it was almost eleven o'clock. She should definitely go up to her room now. If she delayed any longer, Dorothy might return before she did.

She took the elevator to the third floor and half ran, half walked down the hall to 321. She fumbled with her key till she opened the door, and then she quickly locked it behind herself. When she was in her nightgown, she turned off the lights and dove between her crisp sheets. She lay in bed, heart thumping. It was strange to be alone in a dark, unfamiliar room. With all her heart, she wished Dorothy would come back. She listened hard for her sister's footsteps.

The hall was quiet, though, and Emily was tired. As she lay in bed, sleep began to wash over her, wearing her down like waves against a sand castle. The windows were open, and a fresh breeze blew in. *I won't think about ghosts or gangsters or anything else,* she promised herself. *I'll just rest awhile . . .*

Suddenly, an unnatural voice pierced the night. "A drink! A drink!" it demanded.

Emily sat up in bed, trembling. Could someone be in trouble? Was someone sick?

"A drink!" the voice shrieked again. Emily's mind jumped to poor Bridget, who had been left alone to die of typhus. Could this be Bridget's ghost—crying out for water?

Again she heard the strange voice. "Help me!"

CHAPTER 7

HIDING

Emily clutched her blankets, waiting for the voice to cry out again—and desperately hoping it wouldn't. After a few minutes of silence, she heard footsteps in the corridor, then the scraping of a key in the lock.

"Dorothy? Is that you?"

"Of course it's me," Dorothy said. She turned on the light in her room, then walked through to Emily's room. "I came back to get an evening wrap," she explained. "Bitsy and the boys and I are going across the street to the yacht club. We won't be out long."

"No!" Emily protested. "Please don't go out again!"

"Why?" Dorothy asked. "Are you scared of something?"

Emily nodded. "I heard someone crying for help. It was the strangest voice I've ever heard. I . . . I think it was a ghost." Quickly she told her sister the tragic story of Bridget. "Her room was near where we are now," Emily concluded.

Dorothy sat on the edge of Emily's bed. "I don't hear anything. Maybe you were having a nightmare."

"No! I was awake," Emily exclaimed. "Listen."

For a few long minutes, the sisters sat together. Dorothy was beginning to stir restlessly, when the voice came again. "Help me!" it shrieked.

"See?" Emily asked. "I wasn't imagining it!"

Before Dorothy could answer, the voice cried again. "Polly wants a drink!" it demanded, followed by a long, high whistle. "Polly wants a drink! Help me!"

Dorothy laughed. "Silly ninny, your 'ghost' is a parrot!"

Emily was glad the darkness hid her embarrassment. She remembered now that Gwen had mentioned taking care of a parrot. "It *sounded* like a ghost."

Dorothy shook her head. "There's no such thing as ghosts."

"How can you be so sure?" Emily demanded.

Dorothy hesitated. Then she said, "After Daddy died, I prayed for him to come visit me. Every night I prayed for just one visit. I wanted to see him again more than I've ever wanted anything in my whole life." She took a deep breath. "But Daddy never came. So finally I realized that it just isn't possible for someone to come back from the dead. Because if it were, Daddy would have come back to me. I know he would have."

Emily took Dorothy's hand and squeezed it. She felt as if Dot, the sister she loved, was with her again.

Then Dorothy stood up. "So, you'll be all right here on your own for a while, won't you?" she asked briskly.

"I guess so," Emily said reluctantly.

"Good," said Dorothy. "The yacht club is right across the street. We're going to a boat called *The Sleepy Seagull.* Apparently, it's a big boat that has parties just about every night. Chadwick says everybody goes there."

"When do you think you'll be back?"

"Oh, not late," Dorothy replied breezily. "Go to sleep. And stop worrying about everything. We're here to have fun!"

Alone in the dark room, Emily admitted to herself that she'd been wrong at least once tonight. The mystery ghost had turned out to be a noisy parrot. She thought over the events of the day. *Was I wrong about seeing Mr. M, too?*

Sun streamed through the French windows in the morning, and Emily woke early. She looked into Dorothy's room and saw her sister curled up in her blankets. It was barely six o'clock, too early to waken Dorothy. So Emily took out her pencils and drawing paper and quietly stepped out onto her balcony.

The sun glinted over the waves. The morning was clear, and, except for seagulls and a few fishermen, the beach was deserted. *I wish Mother could see this,* Emily thought.

She filled several pages of her sketchbook with scenes of the ocean—a circling seagull, waves crashing on the beach, a fisherman casting his line. Looking out at the sparkling morning, Emily found it easy to believe that all her fears from the previous day must have been imaginary. *Dorothy's right,* she decided. *I should stop worrying and enjoy this beautiful place.*

As the morning stretched on, Emily began to get hungry. Finally, she went into her sister's room. "It's almost eight o'clock. When are we going to get breakfast?"

Dorothy's eyes shot open. "Gad! Breakfast is at nine! Why didn't you wake me earlier? I have to find *something* to wear."

Emily waited while her sister bathed, then tried on and rejected various outfits. Dorothy finally settled on her tan traveling dress as her best outfit for yachting, and the two sisters entered the dining room promptly at nine.

The dining room had been transformed for breakfast. An enormous ice sculpture of a swan stood at the entrance. Instead of red-jacketed waiters, young waitresses in black uniforms served coffee and orange juice. Light streamed in through the tall windows, and fresh bouquets of flowers decorated every table. At the far end of the dining room, where musicians had played the previous night, banquet tables offered a feast of breakfast foods. Guests lined up on both sides of the tables and served themselves from silver chafing dishes.

"It's a buffet," Mrs. Brewster told the sisters as they sat down at her table. "You may help yourselves. If you'd like fried or poached eggs, you may order them from the waitress."

Mrs. Brewster surveyed the dining room. She was wearing fewer diamonds this morning, but she had the same critical expression Emily remembered from last night. "I can't imagine what's keeping Bitsy. The gentlemen are meeting us here this morning."

Emily spotted Bitsy across the room. She was dressed in a white sweater and jaunty white skirt. "There she is," Emily said.

"Where?" Mrs. Brewster and Dorothy asked together.

"Over there," said Emily, remembering just in time that it was rude to point. "By the ice sculpture."

Dorothy peered in that direction for a moment, then laughed. "Bitsy curled her hair! For a moment I didn't recognize her!"

Bitsy came over to the table, smiling exultantly. She twirled in front of her mother. "What do you think?" she asked, fluffing her short blond hair, which was now done in tight curls. "I had Clarice do it up for me this morning. Isn't it just the berries?"

"Very nice," Mrs. Brewster said approvingly. "You look quite different. And, in my experience, gentlemen often find novelty attractive." Mrs. Brewster suddenly broke into a warm smile. "There are your friends now!"

Chadwick and Frank made their way over to the table. This morning, both young men were dressed in sporty white sailing clothes with navy blazers and navy ties. Chadwick also wore a red handkerchief fashionably tucked into his breast pocket. His eyebrows lifted when he saw Bitsy. "I almost didn't recognize you! You look . . ." He struggled for the right word. "Well, you're simply the cat's pajamas!"

Bitsy shone with pride as they all walked up to the buffet together, and Emily felt a pang of sympathy for her sister. Dorothy's tan dress was the best outfit she had for boating, but it didn't compare to Bitsy's sparkling white ensemble. *Dorothy's prettier anyway,* Emily thought loyally. *Even if Bitsy does have nicer clothes and a maid to do her hair.*

As they approached the buffet tables, Emily was almost overcome by the tantalizing smells of crisp fried bacon, fragrant hot yeast rolls, and rich waffles with golden brown maple syrup.

"Don't take too much," Dorothy whispered as Emily loaded her plate with bacon and scrambled eggs. "You can come back for seconds."

But after Dorothy and the others had gone back to the table, Emily added a spoonful of hash brown potatoes to her plate. Then she picked up a pair of silver tongs and piled a blueberry muffin on top of her bacon. A man standing on the other side of the table was helping himself to rolls at the same time. As his hand reached out, Emily caught the glint of a diamond ring on his pinkie finger. She glanced up at his face. The silver tongs dropped from her hand.

It was him! The same man she'd seen on the boardwalk and in the ballroom! Today, he was wearing a white yachting outfit. He looked up at the clatter of the falling tongs, and his gaze met Emily's. His eyes were dark and deep-set and as cold as the bottom of a frozen well. For a second, he inspected Emily as if he thought he'd seen her before— but couldn't quite recall where.

Emily didn't give him time to remember. She grabbed her plate and practically ran back to the Brewsters' table. She took a chair at a corner, where her back would be to the rest of the room. As she placed her plate on the table, her hands were shaking.

Carefully, she turned around and sneaked a glance toward the buffet line. The man was gone. In her mind, she pictured him again—narrow face, deep-set dark eyes, and thin mustache. She was *almost* sure he was Mr. M. He even wore a diamond pinkie ring.

What should I do? she agonized. *Should I tell someone? What if Dorothy only laughs at me again?*

Anxiety wrapped around her stomach like a tight string, and she could only pick at her overflowing plate. Luckily, she did not have to make conversation. Dorothy and her friends were enthusiastically planning their day aboard *Lady Luck*.

"Let's leave right after breakfast," Chadwick urged. He looked over at Emily. "You'd better hurry up and finish eating, Emma, or we'll leave without you." He laughed loudly at his own humor.

"Her name is Emily," Frank corrected him.

"Oh, well—Emily, then." Chadwick laughed again. "Eat up, Emily! We need to get to the yacht club soon."

Emily felt a chill of dread. She didn't want to go anywhere. All she wanted to do was hide from the man with the deep-set eyes. A horrible thought occurred to her: he had been wearing sailing clothes. Maybe he was heading to the yacht club.

She turned to her sister. "I don't feel very well," she told Dorothy in a low voice. "I'll stay here while you go on the boat."

"You're not sick, are you?" Dorothy asked.

"No, just tired. Could I please stay here?"

"All right," said Dorothy. "But you can't go to the beach by yourself. You'll have to stay in the hotel."

Emily readily agreed, and Dorothy announced to her friends that her sister would be staying behind. No one seemed to mind too much. *Dorothy doesn't care,* Emily thought bitterly. *She's happy to be alone with her friends.*

By the time everyone at the table had finished breakfast, the crowd in the dining room had thinned. Emily looked around carefully. The dark-haired man was nowhere in sight. She didn't see him in the lobby either.

He must have left already to go sailing, she told herself.

Dorothy and her friends parted with Emily at the main entrance. "Don't set foot out of the hotel until I get back," Dorothy reminded her in a low voice. "Mother would kill me if I let you go to the beach by yourself."

"I'll stay right here, I promise," said Emily. She quickly said good-bye to her sister and slipped into an empty elevator. "Third floor, please," she told the operator, the glum man she'd seen the day before.

When the elevator reached the third floor, Emily raced to 321. As soon as she was inside, she slammed the door behind her and slid the bolt closed.

Her mind whirled. If the dark-eyed man really was Mr. M, why was he at the Grand Atlantic? She remembered the newspaper story about the witness who had been killed by gangsters. She had witnessed the attack on Mr. Florio. Could Mr. M have followed her here? Was he planning to have her "rubbed out"? She remembered Mr. Florio's warning, "Mr. M is an evil man, *cara.*"

She wished she could turn to Dorothy for help, but she was sure Dorothy would say she was imagining things. *She called me a ninny because I thought the parrot was a ghost. What would she say if I told her Mr. M was staying at the Grand Atlantic?*

Emily sat on the bed, but soon she was up and pacing around the room. Then she went out onto the balcony. She tried to draw scenes of the beach, but all she could

think about was the man with the deep-set eyes. She found
herself sketching his face from memory. When she was
finished, his cold, dark eyes stared at her from the paper.
She shuddered, then crumpled up the sketch and tossed
it into the wastebasket by her dressing table.

As she passed the dressing table, she saw her reflec-
tion in the mirror. She examined it critically. She decided
she was average looking—gray eyes, a nose with a little
bump in the middle, straight teeth, medium-brown braids.
Even if the man is Mr. M, maybe he won't recognize me, Emily
thought hopefully. Then she frowned at herself in the
mirror. *But what if he does?*

She remembered Bitsy's transformation at breakfast.
With her artist's eye for the details of a face, Emily had
recognized Bitsy immediately. But the others, even Bitsy's
mother, had been temporarily confused.

If only I could make myself look completely different,
Emily thought.

Suddenly she had an idea. She grabbed scissors from
Dorothy's sewing kit and hurried back to her dressing
table.

I can't think about it, she told herself, *or I won't have the
courage to do it.* She took a deep breath and closed her eyes.

CHAPTER 8

ROOM 217

Snip! Emily chopped off one braid just below her chin. She felt it fall to the ground like a piece of old rope. She opened her eyes. Her head looked strangely lopsided. *I can't stop now.*

She cut off the other braid at about the same length. Then she brushed her hair out and surveyed the results. It was awfully uneven, especially in the back, where it looked like it had been chewed by a hungry rat. Emily tried to even the edges. The more she cut, the worse it looked.

As she was snipping, a knock sounded at the door. Emily jumped. Had Mr. M tracked her down?

The knock came again.

"Who is it?" Emily asked. She held her breath.

"It's Gwen."

Emily exhaled. "Just a moment!" She grabbed one of Dorothy's hats and pulled it over her hair. Then she opened the door. "Come in."

Gwen was using her braces today. With a step and a swing, she was inside the room. "Milton told me that your sister and her friends went out and that you were up here by yourself," she said. "I thought you might want to come with me while I take care of the pets."

"Milton?" Emily asked. "Who's he?"

"He's the elevator man," Gwen explained. "He was wounded in the war. That's why he sits on a stool."

"Oh," said Emily, recalling the operator's glum face.

"You probably didn't notice him," Gwen continued. "People often don't notice the elevator man. But Milton notices everything. He's a friend of mine, and he's very nice." Gwen paused and looked at Emily curiously. "Why are you wearing your hat backward?"

"It's not really my hat," Emily admitted sheepishly. She took off the hat and shook out her hair. "This is why I put it on."

Gwen's hand flew to her mouth. "Geez!" she exclaimed. "What happened?"

"I decided to cut my hair," Emily explained. "It didn't go very well."

Gwen giggled. "No, I guess it didn't."

Emily drew herself up. "I'm glad you think it's funny."

"Oh, don't get mad," Gwen said, stifling her laughter. "Maybe I can help you fix it. My neighbor's dog has long hair, and in the summer I trim it every few weeks. Mum says I do a good job."

Dog trimming wasn't the best experience in the world, Emily thought, but it was better than nothing. "Well, maybe you can even out the back part," she suggested to Gwen.

Gwen sat on the high four-poster bed, and Emily pulled her chair next to her. For half an hour, Gwen combed and snipped. Finally, she drew back, satisfied. "Look at it now."

Emily approached the mirror cautiously, but she smiled when she saw herself. Her hair was now quite short, an inch or so above her chin, but it was neat, and her curls even looked stylish. "Oh, that's much better! Thank you!"

"You really do look different," Gwen said admiringly. "I like it."

"That's just what I wanted—to look different," Emily said. She glanced at the floor. There were brown curls everywhere. "I'd better clean up."

"I'll help," Gwen offered. As she put a handful of hair into the wastebasket, she saw Emily's discarded sketch. "This is good!" she exclaimed, picking up the sketch and smoothing it out. "Who drew it?"

"I did," Emily said nervously. "I love to draw."

"Geez, I wish I could draw like this. How'd you learn?"

"My mother's an art teacher. She teaches piano, too. I promised her I'd make sketches of the trip." Emily held out her hand for the picture. "But that sketch didn't work out. Let's put it back in the trash."

Gwen, however, was still studying it. "Hey, I know this man. I've seen him somewhere."

"You have? Where?"

"I'm not sure," Gwen said slowly. "It wasn't too long ago, I know that. I remember his eyes. They're dark and kind of scary-looking, just like you drew them. They gave me a start when I looked up and—" Gwen snapped her fingers. "That's it!"

"You remember where you saw him?"

"Yes! It was yesterday, when I went down to take care of Max. This man had golf clothes on, so I guess he was going to the hotel's golf course. He was in an awful hurry. He almost ran into me, and he wasn't very nice about it."

"Do you know his name?" Emily asked urgently.

Gwen wrinkled her forehead. "No, but he came out of the room right next door to the Ramseys. They're Max's owners. They're in Room 219."

"Has he been here long? More than a week?"

Gwen shook her head. "I don't know. Yesterday was the first day I noticed him, but he could have been here longer." She looked at Emily. "Why are you so curious? Is he a friend of yours?"

Emily hesitated. "Can you keep a secret?"

"Cross my heart and hope to die," Gwen said solemnly, making an X over her chest.

"All right," said Emily, and she told Gwen her suspicions about the dark-haired man. She didn't mention the attack on Mr. Florio, because she'd promised Mr. Florio she wouldn't talk about that. But she confided everything else. She began with the sighting of Mr. M in Philadelphia and ended with her encounter with Mr. M—or someone very much like him—at breakfast.

To her great relief, Gwen didn't laugh. Instead, when Emily finished her story, Gwen looked very serious. "Milton said you looked upset when you went to your room this morning. Now I know why. Geez, I'd have been scared, too."

"So you don't think I'm crazy?"

"No," said Gwen. "I told you my Uncle Stuart is manager here at the hotel. I've heard him talk about gangsters who come to the shore. He says they smuggle liquor in from the ocean and cause nothing but trouble. And my brother's Coast Guard ship has stopped lots of smugglers." Gwen paused. "But I never thought a gangster would stay here, at the Grand Atlantic."

"I'm still not one-hundred-percent sure it's Mr. M," Emily admitted. "Maybe I've made a mistake. But I'm scared to leave this room. What if he *is* Mr. M and he recognizes me?"

Gwen nodded thoughtfully. "I know what," she said. "I'll go downstairs. The desk clerk, Nathan, is a friend of mine. He'll tell me who's in Room 217, the room I saw that man come out of. We can see if his name starts with M."

To Emily, it seemed to take forever for Gwen to go down to the lobby and come back. When she finally returned, Gwen said the clerk confirmed that the guest in 217 looked like the man in the picture. "Nathan even remembered his pinkie ring," Gwen said.

"And is the man's name . . ." Emily couldn't quite finish the question.

"He's registered as William W. Wood," Gwen reported. "And he checked in three days ago."

"Three days," Emily repeated. "Are you sure?"

"I checked the date," Gwen assured her.

Emily felt a wave of relief. She and Dorothy had arrived only yesterday. This man, whoever he was, had arrived two days before they did, so he couldn't possibly have followed them. "You're sure his name is Mr. Wood?" Emily persisted.

"Yes," said Gwen. "I saw it on the register myself. Maybe he just looks a lot like Mr. M?"

Emily recalled the man's pinkie ring and the odd inspection he had given her. "I don't know," she said doubtfully. "I suppose it's possible. I can't think of any reason for a man named William Wood to be called Mr. M."

"Well, whatever his name is, he just left to play golf," said Gwen. "Milton saw him go. He'll probably be gone a long time. Want to come take care of the pets with me?"

Emily thought she'd burst if she had to spend much more time alone in the hotel room. And if Mr. M—or Mr. Wood, or whoever he was—had left to play golf, it seemed safe to go out. Still, she decided to be cautious. She exchanged the blouse and skirt she'd put on that morning for her sailor suit. With her new haircut and clothes, she looked quite different from the girl who had gone to breakfast. "I'm ready," she announced.

"First, we'll go upstairs and take care of Madame Serena's parrot," Gwen told her.

The girls took a service elevator to the fourth floor. There were no vases of flowers or Oriental rugs on this floor, but the walls were freshly painted and the floors were clean and polished. Gwen explained that the fourth floor housed staff members. There were apartments for some of the staff, such as the hotel's tennis pro, the bridge teacher, and Madame Serena, and smaller rooms for maids.

"My uncle gave me my own room," Gwen said proudly. "If I'm tired, I can wait up here when Mum works late." Gwen opened the door to a tiny room with a window that overlooked the ocean, a neatly made single bed, and, best of all, a radio.

"The radio was a present from my brother. He gave it to me when I came home from the hospital," Gwen explained. "George and I listen to the Happiness Boys together. They're so funny, they slaughter me!"

As the girls went down the hall to Madame Serena's, they chatted about the Happiness Boys' songs. Gwen was giggling as she unlocked Madame Serena's apartment, but she stopped when she entered. "Geez! Madame forgot to uncover Pauline again!"

The apartment was dark and smelled of perfume mingled with cigarette smoke. Gwen turned on a light, and Emily saw the parrot's cage. It was covered by a tattered plaid blanket and hung near the window. Emily realized that her own room was probably right below the parrot's window. *I bet that's why the voice sounded so close last night,* she thought.

Gwen pulled the blanket off the cage, and a large green parrot blinked at the girls. "A drink!" it cawed. "A drink!"

The girls cleaned Pauline's cage and made sure she had plenty of food and water. "See you later, Pauline," Gwen promised.

"See you later!" Pauline repeated. "See you later!"

The girls' next stop was the bridge instructor's tidy apartment. There they fed and played with the instructor's sleek Siamese cat.

"Now for the guests' pets," said Gwen. The girls went to the second floor, where they picked up the poodle from Room 252 and Max from Room 219.

As they put Max on his leash in the hallway, Emily looked curiously at the door to Room 217. *Was I just imagining that man looked like Mr. M?* she wondered. Aloud, she asked Gwen, "Where do we go now?"

"To the kitchen entrance," Gwen said. "Nobody minds if we walk the dogs there." They went to the entrance where they had talked the previous night and walked the dogs around the driveway. Gwen swung her crutches briskly, but Emily could see that she was sweating from the effort.

"Do you do this every day?" Emily asked.

"Twice a day," Gwen said.

"How do you do it all?" Emily questioned. "I mean, don't you . . ." She stopped, not knowing what to say next.

Gwen glanced at her braces. "You mean these, don't you?" she said matter-of-factly. "When I first got sick with polio, I could hardly move. I was in the hospital a long time. Then I got stronger, and I could use a wheelchair. Now I can walk with braces most of the time. Sometimes I have to go slow, but the animals don't mind." Gwen looked down at the dogs. "Right, Max?" she asked. Max wagged his tail.

"Doesn't it tire you out?"

"Sometimes," Gwen admitted. "But the doctor says the more I exercise, the stronger I'll get. And I like earning my own money. I give half to Mum, and the other half I get to keep. So if I want to go see a movie, I can." She sighed. "I love movies—especially ones with Rudolph Valentino. He's so handsome!"

Emily nodded. She didn't want to tell Gwen that she hardly ever had enough spending money to go to the movies. *I wish Mother would let me take care of pets,* Emily thought. *She doesn't even think I can take care of myself.*

After their walk, the girls took the poodle to its room. Then they returned Max to 219. Again, Emily couldn't help looking at the door of Room 217. *If only I could be sure that man isn't Mr. M,* she thought.

Once they were inside 219, Gwen took off Max's leash and played tug-of-war with him. His tail wagged wildly as he fought her for an old sock. Emily, meanwhile, saw that there was a connecting door between 219 and 217. It was just like the door between the rooms that she and Dorothy shared, except that this connecting door was locked.

The Ramseys had left the key in the lock on 219's side. Filled with curiosity, Emily unlocked the door, took out the key, and peered through the keyhole. The key on the other side blocked her view, and she couldn't see anything. Stepping back, however, she noticed a narrow gap between the bottom of the door and the polished wood floor. She eased herself to the floor and put her eye up to the crack.

Gwen finished playing with Max and put him back into the crate where he slept while his owners were out. Then she looked over at Emily. "What are you doing?"

"I wondered if I could see the room from here," said Emily, a little embarrassed.

Awkwardly, because of her braces, Gwen lowered herself down on the floor beside Emily. "Here," she said, "let me look, too."

Both girls pressed their heads to the floor and peered under the door. The results were disappointing. All they could see was the floor of 217 and the very bottom of some furniture legs.

"Oh, well," said Emily. "I guess it was silly."

As she was about to get up, she heard footsteps in the hall. She grabbed Gwen's hand. Someone was entering 217!

CHAPTER 9
AN UNLOCKED DOOR

A s she lay on the hard floor, Emily felt her heart banging in her chest. She realized that she'd left the door unlocked on 219's side. Whoever had entered 217 could open the door at any time.

More than anything, Emily wanted to get up and run away. But she couldn't. The person in 217 would hear if she or Gwen moved, especially since Gwen's braces creaked. The person would also hear if she turned the key in the lock—and might wonder why it had been unlocked.

All she could do was lie silently and hope no one opened the door. She tried to warn Gwen to be quiet. She lifted her hand carefully and pointed to the unlocked door. Gwen understood immediately. Her eyes met Emily's, and she gave an almost imperceptible nod.

Both girls stayed still and listened. The footsteps next door made a strange clunking noise, and they sounded heavy. Emily felt sure they belonged to a man.

She heard a phone being dialed. A man's voice came clearly under the door. He spoke in a hard, quick voice. "It's me," he said. Then there was a pause.

"Yeah. Give me the numbers," he ordered. As if copying something, he said, "Forty-oh-four by seventy-three-fifty-one, at oh-two hundred. Got it."

Emily repeated the numbers in her head. They sounded like measurements. But for what?

She couldn't quite hear the man's next words. Then, after a pause, he said impatiently, "I told you, everything's arranged for tomorrow night."

The man's next words made Emily's stomach turn. "Hey, remember that kid? The one who skipped town? Guess who's right here at the Grand Atlantic?" He laughed harshly.

"He's got a boat, too," the man continued. "He'll be useful—Lady Luck'll be with us."

The man mumbled something Emily couldn't understand. Then he said, "We're meeting here tonight at midnight. Don't worry. You take care of your side. I'll take care of mine."

The man hung up abruptly. Emily held her breath. She heard the outside door open and then slam. She slipped the key back into the keyhole, and as the man's footsteps faded, she locked the door. Only then did she breathe normally.

"He's wearing golf shoes—I can tell by their sound," Gwen whispered as she pulled herself up. "He's probably going back to the golf course. Let's get out of here."

Emily nodded, too scared to speak. Gwen checked the hall. "It's clear," she whispered. "Let's go to my room!"

As soon as Gwen locked up 219, the girls hurried to the service elevator and took it to the fourth floor. When they were inside the tiny room, Gwen bolted the door. Then she began loosening her heavy leg braces.

"I'm sorry I got you involved in this," Emily told her. "If that man had found us lying on the floor, spying on him . . ."

"Our gooses would have been cooked," said Gwen, finishing the sentence for her. She looked up at Emily, her blue eyes sparkling. "Don't apologize. This is the most exciting thing that's ever happened to me. I wouldn't have missed it for anything!"

Gwen paused and, reaching under her bed, pulled out a tin filled with thick Pennsylvania-style pretzels. "I'm starving, though. I thought for sure my stomach would rumble so loud, that man would hear it." She held out the tin to Emily. "Here, have some."

Emily suddenly realized that she hadn't eaten much breakfast, and it was now past noon. She bit into a crusty pretzel.

"We still don't know much about the man in 217," Gwen pointed out as she crunched. "I couldn't understand what he was talking about. Could you?"

Emily's mouth was dry as she tried to swallow. "I think he was talking about me," she said.

"About you?"

"Yes! Remember when he mentioned the kid who skipped town? Well, I'm a kid and I left Philadelphia— and he saw me this morning."

"He talked about the kid as a 'he,'" Gwen pointed out.

Frowning, Emily tried to remember the conversation. "Are you sure that's what he said?"

"Yes!" Gwen insisted. "He said, 'He has a boat,' or something like that. Then something about luck being with them. So he couldn't have been talking about you."

"What if the 'he' who has a boat is different from the kid who skipped town?" Emily asked. "And the man didn't just say 'luck,' he said 'Lady Luck.' I remember because it made me think of Chadwick's boat." Suddenly, a chilling thought struck her. "Maybe the man was talking about Chadwick!"

"Who's Chadwick?"

"One of my sister's friends. Not the good-looking one—that's Frank."

"Oh," Gwen said immediately. "I know who you mean. I've seen him in the lobby with your sister and her friend. Chadwick's the one who laughs a lot, right?"

Emily nodded. "Mostly at his own jokes."

"Why would the man talk about Chadwick?"

"I don't know," said Emily. "But the man mentioned

a kid and a boat and something about Lady Luck being with them. Chadwick's boat is named *Lady Luck*. Don't you think that's suspicious?"

"Ye-e-es," said Gwen slowly. "But lots of people talk about Lady Luck being with them—it's their way of saying they're lucky. You know, it's possible that this man, Mr. Wood, was just calling someone about business, and he was talking about something being lucky. My uncle makes business calls all the time."

"But why would a businessman plan to meet someone at midnight?"

"That is strange," Gwen agreed. "And I wondered what those numbers meant. Do you remember what they were?"

"I tried to memorize them, but I was too scared," Emily admitted. "All I can remember is forty-something by seventy-three-something. Then I think he said 'oh-two hundred.' I'm not sure of that, though."

"He might have been ordering two hundred of something," Gwen suggested. "Like two hundred pounds of sugar."

"Maybe," Emily said doubtfully. "But why midnight? What if the numbers are a code or something like that?"

Gwen's face lit up with excitement. "Oooooh! Wouldn't it be swell if it was a code? It might take time, but maybe we could figure it out." She glanced at the clock. "Geez! Speaking of time, I've got to go." She began buckling her braces back on. "Mum's leaving early this afternoon. I'll be back tonight after supper. Then we can do more detective work. If the man in 217 is a gangster, we should tell the police!"

Emily felt a stab of fear. It was one thing to sit in Gwen's room and talk about the mysterious man. It was quite another to pursue him. "Maybe we shouldn't do anything more," Emily cautioned as she and Gwen rode down to the third floor on the service elevator.

"We *have* to!" exclaimed Gwen. "We've just begun!" She stepped off the service elevator at the third floor and headed for the main elevators. "Come down to the lobby with me. I'm going to ask Milton what he knows."

Before Emily could protest, Gwen had pushed the elevator button. The first elevator to arrive was operated by a short, stocky man, and he had two passengers with him. Gwen waved him on, telling him she was waiting for someone. As soon as the elevator was gone, Gwen pushed the button again. "I hope there's no one in Milton's car," she muttered.

"We really should be careful," Emily warned her friend. "What if—"

Before she could continue, the doors to Milton's elevator opened. A family of four exited, and Milton was left alone on his stool by the controls. "Going down," he called out. Gwen and Emily slipped inside.

"Milton, I have to talk to you!" Gwen told him as the doors closed.

"Yes?" Milton intoned, his voice as serious as his melancholy expression. "Is there a problem?"

"Remember the man I asked you about—the one in Room 217 who left to play golf? Do you know anything else about him?"

Milton was silent for a moment. Emily was sure that he was going to ask the usual grown-up sort of questions— such as why did Gwen want to know. When he spoke, however, Milton offered only the facts he had observed: The man in 217 often wore yachting clothes in the morning and golfing clothes in the afternoon. Usually, when he went golfing he did not return during Milton's shift, which ended at five o'clock.

"Today, however, I saw that he returned briefly. He went out again carrying his golf bag. I presume he was returning to the golf course."

Emily and Gwen exchanged a glance. "Is there anything else you noticed about him? Anything at all?" Gwen asked.

"He never carries swimming articles, nor does he ever look damp. I presume he does not go bathing in the ocean," Milton reported. "I have never heard him say anything except the number of his floor. Also—" With a gentle thud, the elevator came to a halt on the first floor. Milton paused, his hand on the controls. He looked at Gwen, and his expression became even more somber. "He seems a man who wishes to keep to himself. Leave him alone, Gwen."

The doors opened, and Emily saw several guests waiting

in front of the elevator. She and Gwen exited together. "Going up," Milton called, and the elevator quickly filled. In a moment, the doors closed and Milton was gone.

Emily felt uneasy standing in the main lobby. "Milton's probably right," she whispered to Gwen. "We should just stay away from the man in 217—whoever he is."

"No!" protested Gwen. She turned to face Emily. "We can't listen to Milton. He always worries about me. What if this man really is a gangster and he was talking in code? We could find out what he's doing here. Don't you want to know the truth?"

Emily recalled the thug in Mr. Florio's store. *Don't say nothing to nobody, kid,* he'd warned her. "I'm not sure what I want," she confessed to Gwen.

Another elevator stopped at the lobby level. The operator, the same stocky man they had seen earlier, looked at her. "Going up?"

Emily nodded. "I'd better go back to my room," she told Gwen.

"All right. But we have to find out more," Gwen said firmly. As the elevator door closed between them, she called to Emily, "See you tonight!"

Gwen's parting words chilled Emily. She felt she was being dragged into danger as surely as the elevator was being pulled upstairs. *What have I gotten myself into?*

CHAPTER 10

IN DANGEROUS WATERS

On the way to her room, Emily kept looking over her shoulder to make sure Mr. M wasn't around. When she entered 321, she heard faint noises coming from her sister's room. She called out anxiously, "Dot? Is that you?"

"Who else would it be?" Dorothy asked in strangely muffled tones. Emily hurried into her sister's room and found Dorothy lying, fully dressed, facedown on her bed.

"You're back early," Emily said. "I thought you weren't coming home till four."

"Oh!" groaned Dorothy. She rolled over. Her skin was pale, her eyes were closed, and her hair was a mess. "It felt like we were on that boat for an eternity!" she declared. "I've never been so sick in my life!"

"Seasick?" asked Emily.

"Almost sea-*dead*," moaned Dorothy. "I'll never again

set foot on a boat." She groaned again. "At least not one that's moving."

"Do you want anything? A drink of water?"

Dorothy opened her eyes slightly. "Maybe a small drink of water. I couldn't keep a single thing down on that boat." She paused and looked at Emily more closely. "What did you do to your hair?"

"I cut it," Emily said.

"I can see that. But why?"

Emily paused. She wanted to tell Dorothy everything, but this was not the right time. "I just decided to," Emily said, shrugging her shoulders.

"Mother's going to have a fit," Dorothy predicted. She put her head under her pillow. "But I can't worry about that now. Would you get me that water?"

As Emily was bringing the water, there was a knock at the door. "Dodo, darling!" a familiar voice called. "It's me, Bitsy! Chadwick and Frank and I are going for a swim. Why don't you come with us?"

"Don't let them in," Dorothy whispered to Emily. "They can't see me like this! Tell them I'm not feeling well."

Emily opened the door a crack and gave Bitsy the message. Chadwick and Frank were standing behind Bitsy. Chadwick guffawed loudly. "Not feeling well, huh? Sick as a dog is more like it! Ha, ha, ha!"

Bitsy grinned. "Stop it, Chad!" she exclaimed, poking him playfully with her elbow. "Poor Dodo!"

Chadwick only laughed louder. Frank looked annoyed by his friend, but he said nothing. Bitsy called out over Emily's shoulder, "Sure you wouldn't like a teensy-weensy swim, Dodo? It might make you feel better."

"No, thank you," came Dorothy's muffled reply. "I'll see you later."

"Too bad," Bitsy pouted. "It would have been such fun if we all could have gone together!"

Frank spoke up. "Maybe Emily would like to join us."

Emily was speechless. Ever since she'd seen the ocean, she'd wanted to swim in it. But she never thought that Dorothy's friends would invite her without Dorothy.

"How about it, Emily?" Frank encouraged her. "You know how to swim, don't you?"

"Y-yes," she stammered. "I used to swim in a lake. I've never swum in the ocean, though."

"Just imagine a salty lake with lots of waves. Want to give it a try?"

Emily hesitated. "I—I'd need to get my bathing suit . . ."

"Grab your suit and meet us in the lobby in five minutes," Bitsy told her. Then she looked at Emily closely. "Say, did you do something different with your hair?"

"I cut it," said Emily.

Bitsy smiled triumphantly. "I thought it looked different! See you in the lobby!"

As soon as they left, Emily wondered if she'd made the right decision. What if she ran into the man from 217?

But, she told herself, according to Milton, the dark-eyed man didn't go swimming. He would probably spend the rest of the afternoon on the golf course. And she wanted so much to take a dip in the ocean. Surely she'd be safe, especially if she stayed with Bitsy, Chadwick, and Frank . . .

Emily quickly pulled out her scratchy wool bathing suit. It was the old-fashioned style, and its skirt reached almost to her knees. She knew that among the elegant guests at the Grand Atlantic, her old suit would stick out like a chipped mug in a china tea set. Suddenly, she had an idea.

"If you're not going to swim, could I borrow your bathing suit?" she asked Dorothy. "And a hat?"

Another groan came from under the pillow. Then Dorothy replied, "All right. But take good care of the suit. And don't lose my hat."

Emily put the bathing suit on under her clothes. It was skintight on Dorothy, but it looked baggy on her. Still, Emily thought, it was a big improvement over her own suit, and Dorothy's straw hat shaded her face. *The man in 217 will never recognize me now.*

She met the others in the lobby, and together they left the hotel by the boardwalk exit. Outside, the hot rays of the sun warmed the sand, and a salty breeze ruffled Emily's short hair. She took off her sailor suit in the bathhouse, and then, enjoying the feeling of sand between her toes, she walked with Bitsy toward the water's edge.

The ocean was a bit rough, and most swimmers were

staying close to shore. Frank and Chadwick, however, were bobbing in the water just beyond the breaking waves. Every few minutes, a wave would break early and the boys would either dive underwater or ride the wave toward the beach.

"Come on in," Chadwick shouted to the girls. "The water's fine out here."

Bitsy squealed as the waves lapped at her feet. "Oooh! It's cold!"

Emily remembered the best way to enter cold water. She took a running start and splashed in, diving headfirst into an oncoming wave. She surfaced, laughing. "This is wonderful!" she exclaimed, swimming toward Chadwick and Frank.

The water where the boys were standing was only chest-high for them, but it reached up to Emily's neck. She could touch the sand, though, so she felt secure enough. Bitsy, however, refused to venture any farther than knee-deep water. She called to Chadwick and Frank, "Come back, boys! I don't want to swim by myself."

"I suppose we'd better go back in," Chadwick told Frank. "Bitsy's awfully delicate."

Emily's heart fell. She loved the glorious waves, and she felt too exposed in shallow water. What if Mr. M should walk by and see her? "Can I stay out here?" she asked Frank.

"Come in a little farther," he advised. "Keep in sight of where we're swimming, and watch out for the under-tow. It's strong today."

Emily didn't know what he meant by "undertow," but she nodded anyway. She swam in toward shore until the water reached the middle of her chest. There were more swimmers here, but the water was full of seaweed. Emily rode one wave, then another and another.

Each time she rode a wave toward the beach, she checked to be sure she could see Bitsy, Chadwick, and Frank. Then she dived into the waves and swam out into the surf again. Every time she swam out, however, she found herself going a little deeper to avoid the seaweed. Soon she was swimming in nearly neck-high water again.

I'll be fine out here, she told herself. *I know how to swim. And the waves are much better.*

She was bobbing happily in the cool, blue-green water when a man came swimming toward her, parallel to the beach. She had a glimpse of dark hair and a small mustache. Her heart began to race. She dove into an oncoming wave and swam out, trying to put as much distance as she could between herself and the man. She looked back to see how close he was. He turned his head, and for the first time she saw his face clearly. She felt her whole body relax. It was not the man from Room 217.

The swimmer passed, not even looking in her direction. Emily dove under another oncoming wave and then tried to stand up. She discovered she could barely touch the sand, even on tiptoe. *Time to go in,* she decided.

She started swimming toward shore, but it was more

difficult than she'd expected. Each passing wave seemed to pull her out faster than she could swim in. Soon she couldn't touch bottom at all.

Ice-cold fear began to sweep over her. Then she remembered her mother's parting advice. "If you get into trouble, don't panic. Stay calm and signal for help."

I must stay calm, Emily told herself. *I must.*

Struggling to keep her head above water, she swung her arms in the air, hoping someone would see her. But as she was signaling toward the beach, a wave caught her from behind. It threw her into the ocean. She had to fight to swim up. Finally, she surfaced, her mouth full of salt water.

She barely had time to spit out the water and suck in a breath when another, bigger wave bore down on her. It broke over her, tumbling her head over heels. She ached for air, but she couldn't reach the surface.

Suddenly, something was pulling her upward. Someone was grabbing her arm. She emerged from the water, gasping for breath. When she opened her eyes, she saw Frank's face. "Come on," he ordered, pulling her arm. "You can do it."

Frank was a strong swimmer, and with his help, Emily kicked and pulled her way toward shore. Finally, her feet touched bottom again. She'd never realized how wonderful sand could feel. "Thank you," she told Frank when she was finally standing. "Thank you very much."

"It was nothing," he said, smiling. "I'm on the swim team at college. I saw you waving and figured you'd gotten into trouble. You shouldn't go out so far. The undertow can really pull hard."

"Yes," said Emily, remembering the horrible feeling of being drawn out into the ocean. "I know that now."

Emily dried off on the beach and washed the salty taste of ocean water out of her mouth. Then she joined Bitsy, Frank, and Chadwick as they jumped in the small waves close to shore. Chadwick started to tease Emily. "What were you doing out there underwater?" he asked. "Playing with the mermaids? Ha, ha, ha!"

Emily felt the blood rush to her face. *If Chadwick knew I was in trouble,* she fumed silently, *why didn't he come to help me?*

"She's just a kid, Chad," Frank defended her. "Go easy on her." Bitsy quickly changed the subject.

Soon, they decided they'd had enough swimming. The boys headed back to Chadwick's grandparents', while Bitsy and Emily returned to the hotel. "Tell Dodo we'll see her at dinner," Bitsy said as she stepped off the elevator at the second floor. "There's a dance contest tonight!"

When Emily opened the door to 321, her sister called to her. "Come here for a minute, Em." Emily knew by her voice that something was wrong. She found her sister sitting at her dressing table.

"I have some bad news," Dorothy began.

CHAPTER 11

AN UPSIDE-DOWN CLUE

Emily swallowed hard. "What is it?"

"While you were gone, Mother called, and—"

"Is she all right?" Emily interrupted.

Dorothy nodded. "Yes, but something terrible happened. Last night, someone started a fire in Mr. Florio's store. Mother and Mr. Florio got out in time, and they weren't hurt, but—"

"What about Homer?" Emily interrupted again. "Is he all right?"

Dorothy assured her that Homer was fine. In fact, the dachshund was a hero. It was his barking that had awakened Mother, who in turn had alerted Mr. Florio.

Firemen had been able to save the building, Dorothy said. The store and the apartments, however, were damaged by smoke and by water from the firemen's hoses. Mr. Florio was determined to repair the damage, but it could take weeks. In the meantime, Mr. Florio was living with his sister. Mother was staying with Miss Carter, a fellow teacher who lived nearby.

"Mother said that if there's an emergency and we need to reach her, Miss Carter's neighbors, the Emersons, have a telephone. I wrote down their telephone number."

"Shouldn't we go home?" Emily asked.

Dorothy shook her head. "No, Mother said *definitely* not. She said we shouldn't worry. She wants us to enjoy our vacation."

Emily sat silent for a moment, trying to understand what had happened. "It was the gangsters, wasn't it?" she asked at last. "The ones who threatened Mr. Florio."

"We don't know that for sure," Dorothy replied. She picked up her brush. Turning back to her mirror, she began to smooth her hair. "It could have been someone else, someone who had a grudge against Mr. Florio or—"

"It must be the gangsters!" Emily exclaimed. "They said something bad would happen to Mr. Florio. Then someone sets fire to his store. Who else could it be?" Emily remembered how Mr. Florio had tried to protect his store with a shotgun. He hadn't been prepared for a fire in the middle of the night.

Emily began to pace around the room, thinking about how narrowly Mother and Mr. Florio had escaped. *It's not fair for those gangsters to attack an old man who never hurt anybody! It's not fair for them to destroy our home!*

Then another thought struck her. What if the man in 217 was behind the attack? She decided it was time to confide in her sister.

She took a deep breath and told Dorothy about the man she'd seen at breakfast. "It might be Mr. M," she concluded. "It's definitely the same man I saw on the boardwalk."

"Oh, for heaven's sake," said Dorothy. She put down her hairbrush and faced her sister. "All you think about is gangsters! I admit there are gangsters in Philadelphia; they may even be the ones who set fire to our building. But that doesn't mean there are gangsters lurking around every corner. Especially not here"—she waved her arm around the luxurious room—"at the Grand Atlantic Hotel!"

"But—" Emily began. She was about to tell her sister what she and Gwen had discovered.

Dorothy shook her head. "No buts," she said decidedly. "You're imagining things again. I, for one, am going to take Mother's advice and enjoy our vacation. I suggest you do the same." She turned back to the mirror and picked up her brush again. "Now, please excuse me. I'm going to get dressed for dinner."

Emily retreated to her own room. *I don't care what Dorothy says,* she thought angrily. *I've got to do something.*

At dinner, Emily scanned the tables for the man from Room 217, but the lights were dim and the dining room was full of people. She did not see him anywhere. *Maybe he's gone out,* she thought hopefully. *I wish he'd go away forever.*

When the waiter brought the evening's soup course, he announced it was *vichyssoise.* Emily thought the creamy white soup looked and smelled like Mother's potato soup. She was shocked when she tasted it. It was cold!

She took a few sips of soup just to be polite, then waited for the fish course. When it arrived, she saw that her filet was pink inside. "Is this cooked?" she whispered to Dorothy, who was sitting beside her.

"It's salmon," Dorothy hissed. "It's supposed to be pink."

Emily nodded. But she wondered whether a restaurant that didn't know enough to heat soup could really be trusted to cook fish. She nibbled the pink fish. It tasted as odd as it looked. *The main course will have to be better,* she told herself.

When at last the waiter served the main course, it smelled delicious. "Roast goose!" Chadwick announced with delight. "One of my favorites!"

Emily's stomach turned. *Goose!* she thought. *Oh, no!*

A plate of roast goose with gravy, mashed potatoes, and Brussels sprouts was set in front of her. Emily couldn't help but think about Pepper, the beautiful white goose that had followed her everywhere. She ate a few Brussels sprouts that had not been touched by gravy. Then she put down her fork to signal that she was finished.

Mrs. Brewster saw her full plate and commented about how awful it was when children wasted food.

"Maybe she's too full of seawater to eat her dinner!" laughed Chadwick.

To Emily's surprise, Dorothy came to her defense. "My sister doesn't usually waste food, Mrs. Brewster," said Dorothy, who had barely touched her own plate. "However, we once had a pet goose who was very dear to us." Dorothy then turned the conversation to the big event of the evening, the hotel's all-night dance contest.

Bitsy explained the rules. Dancers would waltz, fox-trot, and Charleston from ten at night till six the next morning, with only two half-hour breaks allowed. Prizes would be given in the morning, with a $50 grand prize for the best dancers. Dorothy, Bitsy, and Chadwick were eager to sign up. Only Frank was reluctant.

"Don't be a wet blanket, Frank," Bitsy urged him. "We're here to have fun."

"I don't know," said Frank, but, under pressure from the others, he finally agreed.

Mrs. Brewster excused herself after dinner. "Must play my bridge!" she trilled. "You young people have fun!"

While Dorothy and her friends were signing up for the contest, Emily went into the lobby. She found Gwen waiting by the front desk. "Come back into the offices," Gwen whispered. "I've found out more about the man in 217."

Gwen led the way to an empty office. She shut the door and pulled a crumpled sheet from her pocket. "I feel like Sherlock Holmes!" she said proudly. "I talked to lots of people on the staff and found four who remembered him."

"What did they say?" Emily asked eagerly.

"First I talked to Ethel," Gwen said, glancing at her notes. "She's a college girl who works as a breakfast waitress. The man from 217 sits at one of her tables. She says he eats alone and always orders poached eggs. He's very picky about his eggs, but he's a good tipper. Tim, one of the bellhops, remembered him and said he has nice luggage. It's monogrammed with his initials, WWW, on top in gold."

Gwen looked at her notes again. "Mr. Adams, the golf pro, says Mr. Wood spends a lot of time on the course, but he's not a very good golfer. Also, Nathan, the desk clerk, said that Mr. Wood arrived here on Saturday, two days before you arrived. He thinks it was August last year when Mr. Wood was here before."

"Oh," said Emily, trying to digest all the information. "Can I borrow some paper?" she asked.

Gwen handed her a sheet of paper, and Emily wrote:

Eats alone
Poached eggs
Good tipper
Monogrammed luggage—WWW
Bad golfer

What does it all mean? she wondered. "He sounds ordinary," she concluded at last. "And I can't think of any reason for Mr. M to have WWW monogrammed on his luggage. Maybe I *was* wrong about him." She shivered slightly. "Still, I wish he wasn't here. I get chills every time I see him. I wonder how long he's staying."

Gwen furrowed her brow. "That's a good question," she said. "I forgot to ask Nathan how long he's registered for. But we could see how long he stayed last year."

"We could?"

"Sure," said Gwen. "The old registers are in my uncle's office. He's gone home for the day, but I bet he wouldn't mind if we looked at them. Come on."

Gwen led Emily through the back of the hotel. They passed the switchboard room, where three women were answering telephone calls and plugging lines into their connections. Gwen ducked her head in. "Mum, this is Emily, the girl I told you about."

A small woman with graying hair and Gwen's bright blue eyes looked up. She took off her headset and greeted Emily cheerfully. "Hello! What are you girls up to?"

"I just wanted to get something from Uncle Stuart's office," Gwen told her mother.

"All right, but don't disturb anything," Mrs. Chapman told Gwen. Then a light flashed on the switchboard. She put her headset back on and said smoothly, "Good evening, the Grand Atlantic Hotel. May I help you?"

Gwen opened the door to her uncle's office, a pleasant, wood-paneled room with two large leather chairs, one on each side of a wide desk. There was a lingering smell of pipe tobacco in the room. It reminded Emily of her father and the pipes he used to smoke. She looked around the office walls, which were lined with bookshelves. "There are so many books! Where is the register?"

Gwen pointed to a black, leather-bound volume on a high shelf. It said *Summer 1924* on its spine. Emily pulled the volume down, and the girls searched through the August listings. Finally they found the entry. William W. Woods had signed in on August 18 and signed out on August 23. He had distinctive, heavy handwriting.

"He only stayed five days last year," Gwen noted. "Maybe he won't stay long this year either."

Emily looked at the entry. "That's odd," she said, pointing to the scrawled signature. "It says 'Woods.' I thought you said his name was 'Wood'—no *s* at the end."

Gwen looked puzzled. "That's what I thought it was." She studied the register for a moment. Then she said, "I'll go to the front desk and check again. I'll be back soon."

She returned ten minutes later. "I saw where he signed himself in this year," she reported. "His handwriting looks the same. But he definitely wrote 'Wood,' not 'Woods,' this year. It could be a mistake, I guess, but it seems awfully strange."

"It does," said Emily. "A person doesn't forget how to

spell his own last name. Unless..."

"Unless he made it up," Gwen finished for her. "And he doesn't remember how he spelled it before. 'Wood' or 'Woods'—if it wasn't his real name, it's easy to see how he could make the mistake."

The girls sat opposite each other at Mr. Chapman's wide desk and considered various ideas. Was the misspelling just a careless error? Or could Mr. Wood/Woods have registered under a false name? Was he actually Mr. M?

"Remember his monogrammed luggage?" Gwen recalled. "Why would Mr. M have luggage monogrammed WWW?"

"I don't know," Emily confessed. She began doodling absentmindedly on the scrap paper. First, she sketched a suitcase. Then, on a corner of the paper, she drew three block-letter W's.

"Geez!" Gwen exclaimed. "Look!" Gwen turned the paper around.

Suddenly Emily was staring at three M's.

"That could explain the monogrammed luggage," Gwen said solemnly. "I think Mr. Wood—or Woods—could be your Mr. M. We'd better find out what he's doing here."

CHAPTER 12

WAITING IN THE DARK

"If the man in 217 *is* Mr. M, he's very dangerous," Emily warned her friend. She told Gwen how Mr. Florio's store had been set on fire the previous night. "I'm sure the gangsters set the fire," Emily concluded. "And Mr. M is the gangsters' boss."

"But why is he here in Shell Cove?" Gwen persisted. "We know he didn't follow you here."

"Maybe he's planning something," Emily suggested. "He could be using that code we heard to talk about it."

"He might have a deal with rumrunners," Gwen said thoughtfully. "That would explain why he'd be here. Rumrunners like our coast because we're close to New York and Philly. The gangsters can buy their liquor here, then take it to the cities."

"Why would he stay at the hotel?" Emily asked. "Wouldn't he just buy the liquor and leave?"

"He could be waiting for his shipment to arrive,"

Gwen said. "And if he *is,* I could tell my brother."

Emily was confused. "Your brother? What could *he* do?"

"He's a Coast Guard officer," Gwen said, as if explaining the obvious. "His ship patrols the waters, looking for rumrunners. If George knew a big shipment was coming, especially if he knew when and where, he could arrest the rumrunners—including Mr. M."

"But we're still not sure that's what Mr. M is doing," Emily pointed out.

"True," Gwen agreed. "I wish we knew more."

For several long minutes, the girls sat silently. Finally Gwen said casually, "You know, Max's owners, the Ramseys, have signed up for the dance contest tonight. They'll be gone all night. They asked me to look in on Max."

"So?" asked Emily.

"So, Mum's working the late shift tonight. And your sister will be at the dance contest. She wouldn't know if you weren't in your room at midnight."

Emily looked at her. "You don't mean..."

Gwen's blue eyes flashed. "Yes! Mr. Wood—or whatever his name is—said he was meeting someone tonight at midnight. We could wait in Room 219 and listen to their meeting. Then maybe we'd find out what's going on."

Emily remembered how terrified she'd felt as she lay on the cold wood floor, listening to the man in 217. She shook her head. "No, we can't do that again," she said. "I was scared half to death."

"We'd be smarter this time," Gwen urged. "We'd make sure the door was locked on our side."

"What if the Ramseys come back to their room early?" Emily objected. "What would we do then?"

"One of us could stay in the lobby and watch for the Ramseys," Gwen suggested. "We could have a signal. Two phone rings could mean 'Get out of the room fast.'"

Emily bit her lower lip. The very thought of being near Mr. M gave her shivers, but she *had* to do something to stop the gangsters. "All right," she said finally. "I'll go. Will you let me into 219?"

"No," said Gwen, surprised. "*I'll* be the one in 219. You wait in the lobby."

Emily was tempted by this plan. But after a moment, she shook her head. "No, I should be the one to wait in 219, not you."

Gwen flushed to the roots of her red hair. "Why?" she demanded angrily. "Just because I wear these"—she gestured at her braces—"doesn't mean I can't be a good detective. Besides, it was *my* plan, and *I'm* the one who has the keys to the room."

"I wish you *could* be the one to go," Emily admitted. "But it makes more sense for me. Your braces are noisy—and so is the wheelchair. What if the man in 217 heard you? How could you make a fast getaway?"

"What am I supposed to do?" snapped Gwen. "Sit around and do nothing?"

"You'd be much better at watching the Ramseys than I would," Emily pointed out. "If I stood around in the lobby, people would wonder what I was doing there. No one would pay much attention to you—they'd think you were waiting for your mother. And you could get your mother to place the signal call if we needed it. How would I do that?"

"I don't know, but—" Gwen began.

"Besides," Emily interrupted, "you may have the keys, but I'm the one who recognized Mr. M—and I'm the one whose apartment was set on fire."

The flush of anger gradually faded from Gwen's freckled face. "All right," she agreed at last. "I'll watch for the Ramseys. But you'd better tell me everything Mr. M says!"

Emily didn't want to risk seeing Mr. M, so she stayed in the office area while Gwen walked the dogs. As she waited for Gwen to return, Emily kept remembering the witness who was killed by gangsters because he knew too much. *I must have been crazy to tell Gwen I'd spy on Mr. M,* she thought nervously. *Why did I say yes?*

Emily had almost decided to call the whole plan off when Gwen returned to the office, her eyes shining with excitement. "I asked one of the night elevator operators to keep an eye out for Mr. Wood for me," she reported. "I told him that Mr. Wood yelled at me once and I didn't want to run into him again, which was mostly true."

"Has he seen him?"

Gwen nodded. "He said Mr. Wood—or whatever his name is—left the hotel about half an hour ago. He got into a car, so he should be gone awhile. Are you ready?"

Emily took a deep breath. She desperately wanted to back out, but she knew in her heart that she couldn't. "Yes, I guess so."

Together, she and Gwen took Max to 219. They threw a ball for him until he was tired of chasing it. He settled into Gwen's lap, content to be petted. "I suppose I should put him in his crate now and go downstairs," Gwen said reluctantly. "It's past eleven."

After Max was in his box, the girls turned off all the lights except one small bedside lamp. "Remember, the signal is two rings," Gwen said as she left.

"I'll remember," promised Emily.

"Good luck!" Gwen whispered. Then she headed down the corridor. Emily listened to her *step, swing, step, swing* until the noise faded away.

Alone in the darkened room, Emily made sure the connecting door to 217 was locked. As she settled herself by the door, she heard Max whine. She looked over and saw him watching her from between the slats of his crate. He wagged his tail hopefully.

"All right," Emily said softly. "I'll let you out. But you'll have to be quiet."

She released him from his crate, and he quickly curled up in her lap. The room was eerily quiet, and she was glad of Max's company. There was a clock on the Ramseys' dresser, and Emily watched the minute hand. It seemed to move so slowly that she wondered whether it was broken. The room felt cold and lonely. *I wish I were anywhere but here,* she thought despairingly. *Why couldn't I have stayed home in Philadelphia?*

Then she remembered that fire had wrecked her home. *If I had stayed in Philadelphia, I might have been killed,* she realized. It was a terrifying thought. For a moment she sat motionless in the darkened room.

As soon as she stopped petting him, Max stood up, demanding attention. "Oh, Max," she whispered, scratching the little dog behind the ears. "What am I going to do? I'm so scared."

The telephone jingled loudly. Emily anxiously counted the rings. *One . . . two . . .* When it rang a third time, she sighed. She half wished it *had* been a warning call from Gwen. Then she would have had a good excuse to abandon her spy mission.

She returned to watching the slow-moving clock. Just before midnight, she heard footsteps entering Room 217. *This is it!* Emily told herself. She felt her heart throbbing behind her ribs. She quietly stretched out on the floor so that her ear was near the crack at the bottom of the door.

Max made it clear that he didn't like her new position. He nudged his nose into Emily's face, urging her to sit back up. She wished she'd put the little dog back in his crate, but it was too late for that now. She stroked his back until he settled on the floor next to her. She waited tensely. For a few minutes all she heard was the man moving around his room. Then there was a knock on the door, and another person entered 217.

"I have the cash," said a young man's voice. He spoke so quietly, Emily had to strain to hear him. "Here it is, five hundred dollars."

"You owe me interest," the man from 217 replied. His voice was loud and commanding.

"That's all I have . . . I had to . . ." The young man's voice was low. Emily couldn't quite make out all the words, but she had the impression that the speaker was educated. And his voice sounded familiar.

"You don't have to get more money," the man from 217 said. "All you gotta do is take that fancy boat of yours on a little trip tomorrow."

"I can't," the young man began. The rest of his sentence faded away.

I've heard that voice before, Emily thought. *But where?*

"I don't care about your problems," the man from 217 said. "You're going to take *Lady Luck* out tomorrow night and meet up with two other boats outside the harbor at eleven o'clock. I'll tell you the rest of the job then."

Lady Luck! thought Emily. Suddenly she felt sick to her stomach. The other voice *must* be Chadwick's. But what business would Chadwick have with this man?

"I paid you the money I owe," the young man said. "If you want interest, I can get you twenty-five dollars by tomorrow or—"

The voice of the man from 217 turned icy. "I'm not asking you. I'm telling you: If you're not out there at eleven tomorrow night, my boys'll come looking for you— and your girlfriend, too."

Emily's heart lurched. *Girlfriend! He must mean Bitsy!*

"I'll be there," the younger man said shortly.

The door shut. Emily, her mouth dry with fear, realized the meeting must be over. She began to edge away from the connecting door. She tried to creep as silently as she could, but Max, seeing her crawling on the floor, thought she wanted to play. He jumped excitedly.

"Not now, Max!" she whispered.

She had covered almost ten feet when the phone in the next room rang shrilly. The closet was standing open beside her. Startled, she dove behind its louvered doors. She huddled among the Ramseys' shoes and hanging clothes, shaking with fear.

Pressed against the closet wall, she could hear the one-sided conversation in the next room. The man in 217 seemed to be arranging the next night's meeting.

"I'll go with you," he told the caller. "Crosby will take Harris on his boat, and the kid'll go by himself. We'll take different routes to the ship."

He seemed to listen for a minute. Then he said, "Yeah,

we got the numbers. They're going to come a little inside the limit so we can meet 'em. They'll be at forty-oh-four latitude, seventy-three-fifty-one longitude. We meet at the ship at oh-two hundred hours."

Emily repeated the numbers in her head, making sure that this time she remembered them. *So "oh-two hundred" is hours,* she thought. *I wonder what that means?*

"This'll be the biggest shipment yet," the man from 217 bragged. "Our boat and Crosby's will take most of the crates. We'll go first, and Crosby'll go second. We'll have the kid loaded last." The man laughed harshly. "He thinks his boat is fast, but it's nothing compared to ours. If the Coast Guard comes after us, he'll be the one they catch."

Emily felt a pang of sympathy for Chadwick. She had never really liked him, but it seemed he was being led into a dangerous trap. *How did he ever get mixed up with these people?*

The man from 217 laughed again. "Yeah, we'll be lucky all right," he boasted. "As my mother used to tell me, 'Michael, you got to make your own luck.'"

Michael! The name turned Emily cold. The man in the next room had to be Mr. M! She'd heard all she could stand. She opened the closet door, hoping to make her escape. But Max was outside the closet, eagerly waiting for her. He became so excited, he started running around in circles. His tail knocked over a glass on a low table. It banged noisily, then shattered on the floor.

Terrified, Emily jumped back into the closet, closing the louvered doors behind her. A voice called out from 217. "Hey! Who's there?" Emily clamped her mouth tight to keep her teeth from chattering.

The man from 217 knocked loudly on the connecting door, but Emily stayed silent. *The door is locked,* she told herself. *I'm safe in here.*

Then she heard a scratching noise from the connecting door. It took her a moment to realize what was happening. Suddenly she understood—and all her confidence vanished. The man from 217 was picking the lock!

CHAPTER 13
A TRAP

Crouched in the closet, Emily felt squeezed by fear. She could barely breathe. *Please don't let him find me here,* she prayed. *Please!*

Suddenly, the connecting door opened. Through the slats of the louvered door, she watched Mr. M enter the room. He had something in his hand. Emily crouched lower behind the door, hardly able to believe what she saw—he was holding a gun.

Max saw Mr. M, too. He knew instantly that this man was an intruder. Barking ferociously, he ran headlong toward the stranger.

Mr. M cursed the little dog and kicked at him. Max dodged just in time, then retreated to the other end of the hotel room, still barking wildly.

The gangster surveyed the half-lit room and noticed the broken glass on the floor. "Stupid animal," he muttered. Then he turned and went back to his room, closing and locking the connecting door.

Emily was trembling, but she couldn't stay in the room any longer. As Max continued to bark wildly, she sprinted for the hall door and opened it a crack. The hallway looked empty. She quietly closed the door to 219 behind her. Then she ran through the hall and down the curved staircase to the lobby. She didn't stop running till she found Gwen sitting in one of the lobby's armchairs. "We have to go someplace safe to talk!" she said breathlessly. "Quick!"

Gwen led the way to her uncle's office. "What happened?" she demanded as soon as the door was locked behind them. "What did you find out?"

"I'll tell you in a minute," Emily said. She grabbed a piece of scrap paper. "I have to write these numbers down." She copied the information Mr. M had given over the phone: 40-04 latitude, 73-51 longitude.

"There," she said, passing the paper to Gwen. "The numbers weren't a code at all. They're directions. That's where they're going."

"Who?" asked Gwen. "Where? What do you mean?"

Emily told Gwen everything that had happened. "You were right," she concluded. "Mr. M *is* a rumrunner. He's planning to bring crates of liquor in by boat. He said the shipment is going to be his biggest ever."

"Geez!" exclaimed Gwen. She looked at the numbers

in her hand. "The ship probably radioed its location to someone on the coast," she said slowly, "and that person called Mr. M here at the hotel." She looked up at Emily. "Now Mr. M knows where the ship will be tomorrow night—and we know where Mr. M will be. I wish we knew what time they were meeting."

"Mr. M said something about 'oh-two hundred hours.' I'm not sure what he meant. Maybe something's happening in two hundred hours?"

Gwen stared at her, and an expression of disbelief passed over her face. "No! That's not what it means. Oh, I was so stupid!"

"About what?"

"Oh-two hundred hours is the military way of telling time," explained Gwen. "Instead of one o'clock, two o'clock, they say oh-one hundred hours, oh-two hundred hours, and so on, all the way through twenty-four hundred, which is the same as midnight. Sometimes my brother talks that way. He'll tell me he'll pick me up at eighteen hundred hours. That means he'll be here at six P.M."

"So oh-two hundred hours is two A.M.?"

"Right," Gwen said. "Now we know where the smugglers will be and when they'll be there. We can have them arrested."

"We *can't* go to the police," Emily protested. "Mr. Florio told me some police are in with the gangsters. If we talk to the police, one of them might tell Mr. M we were spying on him. And then . . ." Emily stopped, remembering the gun in Mr. M's hand.

"I think the policemen around here are honest," Gwen said, frowning. "But I wasn't going to go to them anyway. I'll go straight to my brother. He'd never tell anyone where he got the information. And he'll warn the Coast Guard, so they can catch Mr. M tomorrow night." Gwen smiled at Emily. "With Mr. M gone, maybe your neighborhood'll be safe again."

Emily tried to return her friend's smile, but another worry was gnawing at her. "What should we do about Chadwick?"

"What do you mean?"

"From what I heard, it sounds as if Chadwick doesn't want to help Mr. M, but he's being forced into it. I don't like Chadwick much, but he's a friend of Dorothy's. I wish I could warn him."

"That's impossible," said Gwen. "If Chadwick is in cahoots with the gangsters, how could we trust him not to pass your warning on to Mr. M?"

Emily realized that she didn't know Chadwick very well. If he was willing to work with gangsters, what else might he do? "I guess we couldn't," she admitted.

"If he told Mr. M, the trap would be ruined," Gwen continued. "And what about the Coast Guard crew? My brother and his shipmates would be put in danger. Besides, didn't Mr. M say that if Chadwick didn't show up, they'd come after him—and his girlfriend?"

"Yes," said Emily. "Poor Bitsy!"

"If the Coast Guard catches Chadwick smuggling, he'll go to jail—but at least he'll be alive," Gwen reasoned. "And so will Bitsy. But if the gangsters go after them, who knows what will happen?"

Emily sighed. "I guess you're right," she said reluctantly.

Just then a voice called from the hallway. "Gwen? Are you in there?"

"Yes, Mum," Gwen answered. She opened the door and Mrs. Chapman came into the office. She looked tired, but she was smiling. "Goodness, girls!" she exclaimed. "You're up late. Time for us to go home, Gwen."

Emily walked with Gwen and her mother back to the lobby. Even at this late hour, elegantly dressed couples were laughing and talking under the lobby's glittering chandelier. Emily was relieved to see that Mr. M was nowhere around.

Near the elevators, she said good-bye to Gwen and Mrs. Chapman. "I'll see you tomorrow," she said, giving Gwen a significant glance.

"Good-bye," said Gwen, adding in a low tone, "I'll take care of everything, just like we talked about."

As she turned to go up to her room, Emily heard music and cheering at the other end of the lobby. A dozen couples from the dance contest had spilled out of the ballroom and into the north end of the lobby. The dancers were swinging to the Charleston while onlookers encouraged them. "Get hot! Get hot!" the spectators called out.

Emily spotted her sister. She and Frank were dancing in the midst of the crowd, while Bitsy and Chadwick were swaying together nearby. Dorothy was kicking her heels high, and her face was glowing with happiness.

For a moment, Emily felt sorry for her sister. *I'm glad she's having fun tonight,* she thought. *She'll feel terrible when she hears about Chadwick.*

Emily was frightened to be alone in her room that night, but she was so tired that sleep overcame her fear. When she woke up, the sun was streaming in. She heard familiar footsteps in the next room.

"Dorothy?"

Dorothy stepped through the connecting door, a towel wrapped around her head. "Good morning! Sorry for waking you up, but I just *had* to take a bath before I go to bed."

"Go to bed?" Emily echoed. "Did you just get in?"

"Yes!" Dorothy exclaimed. "They judged the all-night contest at six this morning, and guess what?"

"What?"

"Frank and I won!" Dorothy announced. "I've never danced so much in my life. My feet are killing me! But Frank is a marvelous dancer and we had the best fun.

And this morning, after it was all over, Bitsy convinced me to play the grand piano in the lobby. I don't know what came over me, but I said yes. So there I was, playing in the lobby, and a whole crowd of people gathered. We were singing up a storm, till the manager came out. He said he loved the music, but we might wake other guests, so we had to stop." She laughed delightedly at the memory. "Oh, well, we can sing some more tonight! And guess what?"

"What?"

"First prize was fifty dollars. Frank and I split it in half, so now I have twenty-five dollars! Hurrah!" Dorothy began to comb out her wet hair. "It was absolutely the best dance contest ever," she gushed. "Everyone had fun, even Bitsy and Chadwick, and they didn't win a prize."

"What do you think of Chadwick?" Emily asked, trying to sound casual.

Dorothy shrugged. "He can be a little annoying," she admitted. "But Bitsy likes him, and he and Frank are fraternity brothers at college, so I guess he's all right. Why do you ask?"

Emily hesitated. She wanted to warn Dorothy, but she had to be careful not to tell her too much. Finally, she said, "I'm sorry to have to tell you this, but Chadwick is involved with gangsters."

To Emily's surprise, Dorothy laughed loudly. "Gangsters! You must be joking!"

"No, I'm not joking," said Emily, hurt. She wondered how she could make Dorothy believe her. "I, uh, overheard Chadwick talking to a man," Emily began, choosing her words carefully. "Chadwick had borrowed five hundred dollars from the man, and the man wanted Chadwick to do something illegal. He said if Chadwick didn't do it, he'd get into big trouble."

Dorothy stared at her. "Are you crazy? Chadwick has no reason to borrow money from anybody. He's rich! That's why Bitsy's mother likes him so much! His family has barrels of money."

"Are you sure?" Emily asked, stunned.

"Of course I'm sure," Dorothy said. "In fact, just the other day, Chadwick loaned Frank five hundred dollars. Chadwick didn't care—he even joked about it. Money means nothing to him."

"Oh," said Emily. She could just imagine Chadwick's jokes. *Could I have been wrong?* she wondered.

Dorothy came and sat down on the bed beside her. "Look, Em, I'm starting to worry about you. You imagine gangsters everywhere you go."

I'm not imagining! Emily wanted to scream. But she said nothing.

"I guess it's partly my fault," Dorothy continued. "You've been alone a lot on this vacation, and I'm sorry." She paused, then said, "Hey, I know what. Later, why don't you and I go down to the boardwalk together? I've got an extra twenty-five dollars now, and I can buy us treats. We can even ride the carousel! Would you like that?"

Emily nodded, but her mind was racing. What if Dorothy was right? What if it *wasn't* Chadwick who'd been talking to Mr. M last night? She'd been sure she recognized the voice. A horrible idea occurred to her. "Dorothy," she asked, "was Frank with you all last night at the dance contest?"

"Of course," said Dorothy. She stood up from the bed and started combing her hair again. "We were partners."

"Yes, but did he leave at all—any time?" Emily insisted.

"Well, he took a break just before midnight—Chadwick and Bitsy teased him and called him Cinderella. But he was back in less than fifteen minutes." Dorothy looked at her probingly. "Why do you ask? This isn't another one of your crazy theories, is it?"

"No," Emily replied, "I was just curious." She covered her head with a pillow so that Dorothy couldn't read her eyes. *It must have been Frank I heard—not Chadwick!*

She wished she could confide in Dorothy, but she was no longer sure she could trust her sister. Would Dorothy even believe her? And, if she did believe, would she then warn Frank?

"I'm going to bed now," Dorothy announced, yawning. "Bitsy wants us all to go back to *The Sleepy Seagull* tonight,

so it may be another late night. You go down to breakfast
without me. Give Mrs. Brewster my apologies."

At nine o'clock, Emily entered the dining room carefully, watchful for Mr. M. *I feel like a mouse coming out of
its hole,* she thought. *I just hope the cat isn't waiting to pounce
on me.*
Scanning the dining room, she saw it was relatively
uncrowded. A lot of people had decided to sleep in after
the dance contest, Emily guessed. She did not see Mr. M.
She hoped that he'd decided to sleep in, too.
Mrs. Brewster was sitting alone at their table, a crossword puzzle set out in front of her. She nodded as Emily
gave her Dorothy's excuse. "Well, be sure to eat everything you take on your plate this morning," Mrs. Brewster
said as she bit into a heavily buttered roll. "I hate to see
children waste their food." Mrs. Brewster then turned her
attention back to her crossword and ignored Emily for the
rest of the meal.
Although she was hungry, Emily decided not to go up
to the buffet. She didn't want to risk coming face-to-face
with Mr. M again. Instead, she ordered fried eggs from
the cheerful young waitress who came to the table serving
coffee and juice. While she waited for her order, Emily
couldn't help checking the dining room again for Mr. M.

She didn't see him, but her anxiety grew. *What will happen if I meet him again?* she worried.

By the time her plate arrived, Emily had lost her appetite. Only the thought of another reprimand from Mrs. Brewster convinced her to eat the perfectly fried eggs and the triangles of buttered toast that accompanied them. Her stomach churned every time she thought about Frank. *He's been so nice to me, and he saved my life in the ocean,* she thought. *How can I send him into a trap?*

Then another thought struck her. When Mr. M had threatened the girlfriend, it was Dorothy he'd been talking about, not Bitsy. *Dorothy's in danger,* Emily realized, *and she doesn't even know it!*

CHAPTER 14

A STRANGER'S FACE

After breakfast, Emily looked into the lobby. She checked to be sure Mr. M was nowhere in sight. Then she went to the front desk to look for Gwen. The desk clerk told her that she'd just missed her friend. Gwen had cared for the pets earlier in the morning, then gone to a doctor's appointment.

Emily's heart fell. "She's already left?"

The clerk said yes, but he added that Gwen's mother, Mrs. Chapman, would be on duty in the evening. Gwen would be back then.

Emily thanked him and walked back through the lobby, still keeping a careful eye out for Mr. M. As she headed toward the elevators, she saw a broad-shouldered, balding man with a handlebar mustache. He was sitting in one of the lobby armchairs with a newspaper open in front of him. Emily noticed, however, that he wasn't reading the paper. Instead, he was surveying the hotel, as if he was looking for someone.

She watched him as he watched the lobby. She knew she'd seen his face before, but she couldn't remember where. *Could he be a member of Mr. M's gang?* she wondered. *Or am I imagining gangsters everywhere?*

Emily hurried back to her room, shut the door, and turned the bolt. She checked on her sister in the next room. Dorothy was still sound asleep.

With a sigh, Emily stepped onto the balcony. A warm breeze was blowing, and the sky was aquamarine blue. The surf was calmer today, and she could see dozens of swimmers jumping in the waves. Emily wished she could join the swimmers. She imagined how refreshing a cool dip in the ocean would feel. But she knew Mr. M could be on the boardwalk. He might even venture onto the beach. She decided she would stay behind the hotel room's locked door.

She remembered, though, how easily Mr. M had picked the lock to Room 219. *I wonder,* she thought, *if I'll ever feel really safe again.*

Dorothy slept until noon. She was awakened by a call from Bitsy. "Good morning!" Bitsy chirped. "I'm coming right up. You'll never guess what's happened!"

A few minutes later, Bitsy appeared at Dorothy's door. She was wearing an expensive but very conservative navy dress and white gloves. Her hair was smooth, and her only makeup was a tiny bit of lipstick. "Guess what!" she announced.

"What?" replied Dorothy, who was still in her nightgown.

"Chadwick's grandparents have invited us to their cottage for tea! Isn't that exciting? You'll have to get ready quickly!" She lowered her voice. "I think Chadwick wants to see if they'll approve of me as the future Mrs. Chadwick Wellingsford!" Bitsy twirled in front of them. "What do you think?"

"Very nice," said Dorothy. "By the way"—she gave a significant glance toward Emily—"are we all invited?"

Bitsy shrugged. "I guess so," she said without much enthusiasm. "If she'd like to go."

"I'd rather not, thank you," Emily said hastily. "I, uh, have a headache."

"Maybe you *should* come," said Dorothy, looking concerned. "You might feel better if you keep busy."

"No, thanks," Emily told her sister. "I'll just lie down for a while. Then maybe I'll read or draw."

"We won't be gone long," Bitsy piped up. "We'll be back in time for dinner. Hurry up and get dressed, Dodo! Chadwick's coming to pick us up soon! I'll meet you in the lobby."

Dorothy quickly did her hair and then put on a pretty yellow dress and her best white gloves.

"Why are you and Bitsy getting so dressed up for tea at a cottage?" Emily asked.

"I told you Chadwick's family is rich," Dorothy said as she fastened on a pearl circle pin that she'd borrowed from Mother. "Rich people talk differently than we do. What they call a cottage is actually a mansion, and their teas are formal afternoon parties." She squinted at herself in the mirror. "I hope I look all right."

She turned to Emily. "I guess we'll have to go to the boardwalk tomorrow. Don't leave the hotel while I'm gone," she warned. "I'll be back before dinner."

The afternoon crawled by for Emily. Alone in the room, she read, sketched, and imagined all the fun things she would do if she could join the vacationers on the beach.

She also imagined everything that might go wrong if tonight's plan failed. *What will I do if Mr. M is still here tomorrow?* she worried. *I can't hide forever.*

And if the plan did succeed, Frank would probably be caught too, Emily realized. She remembered Frank's kind smile, how he had pulled her out of the ocean, and how he'd defended her against Chadwick's teasing. She wished she could help him. But she couldn't think of any way to warn Frank without putting other people in danger.

Dorothy returned just before dinner. "The cottage is beautiful," she reported to Emily as she changed out of her tea dress and into her evening gown. "It's a huge mansion right on the sea. But all they had to eat were tiny cucumber-and-watercress sandwiches. I'm starved!"

Emily could sympathize; she had missed lunch completely. Together, the two sisters went down to dinner. As they walked into the candlelit dining room, Emily felt relieved when she surveyed the room and did not see Mr. M. Still, to be on the safe side, she chose a corner seat at Mrs. Brewster's table so that her back would be to the other diners. *Even if Mr. M does come in*, she told herself, *maybe he won't see me.*

Dinner was delicious. The soup was cream of tomato, and it was properly hot. There was flounder for the fish course, and roast beef with Yorkshire pudding for the main course. Dessert was vanilla ice cream with hot caramel sauce.

Under Mrs. Brewster's critical eye, Emily ate everything on her plate. She would have enjoyed it much more, however, if Frank and Chadwick hadn't been there. Whenever she looked at Frank, Emily worried, *Am I sending him to prison?*

Frank seemed preoccupied, too. Bitsy, Chadwick, and Dorothy joked all through dinner, but Frank looked serious. When the others discussed their plan for the evening— visiting *The Sleepy Seagull* at the yacht club—Frank was not enthusiastic. "Maybe I'll skip *The Sleepy Seagull* tonight," he said.

Bitsy coaxed and persuaded him until he finally agreed to go along. "I'll have to leave early, though," he warned.

"Frank's taking *Lady Luck* out tonight by himself," Chadwick announced. "He wants to prove what a great fisherman he is."

"You're going by yourself?" Dorothy asked. "Isn't that dangerous?"

"I used to go out on Lake Erie by myself all the time," Frank said with a shrug. "Besides, I've heard the fishing here is best at night."

Emily stared down at the white linen napkin in her lap. Any doubts she'd had about Frank were now gone. *He must be the one,* she thought. She could hardly stand to look at his face.

After dinner, Emily saw Gwen waiting for her near the front desk. The girls found a quiet corner of the lobby behind a large pillar. There they could see people passing by without being seen themselves. In a whisper, Gwen assured Emily that everything was ready. "The Coast Guard will be at Mr. M's meeting place tonight. They'll trap him there—and they'll get anyone with him, too."

"There's a problem," Emily whispered back. She explained to Gwen that it was Frank, not Chadwick, that she had heard talking to Mr. M.

"Geez!" Gwen exclaimed. "I always thought Frank seemed nicer than Chadwick!"

"He *is* nicer," Emily agreed. "He saved me from drowning in the ocean. And I think Dorothy's in love with him. How can I let him go into a trap?"

"But you can't warn him—not now!" Gwen insisted.

Emily knew Gwen was right. Yet she felt like a traitor for betraying Frank. *I wish there was some way I could help him,* she thought. *But how?*

As she and Gwen stood together in the lobby, Emily saw the muscular, balding man with the handlebar mustache whom she'd noticed earlier. He was walking toward the hotel offices. Emily stared at him.

"Gwen," she whispered, "see that man over there? The one with the mustache? Do you know who he is?"

Gwen hesitated. Then she shook her head.

"I've seen him before," Emily said. "I think he could be one of the gangsters."

Gwen's freckled pink cheeks went pale. "No," she said. "No, you're wrong!"

Emily was puzzled by her friend's reaction. "I know his face," she insisted. "Who is he?"

Gwen looked around the crowded lobby. "Let's go in the back," she suggested. They entered the office area, and Emily saw the man with the mustache going into Mr. Chapman's office. She stared at him, and a picture flashed into her mind: the newspaper photo of the federal agents raiding bootleggers. The man with the mustache had been half smiling at the camera.

"His picture was in the newspaper," she told Gwen excitedly. "He's a federal agent!"

"Shhh!" Gwen hushed her. "No one's supposed to know! Promise you won't tell?"

After Emily promised, Gwen explained that the man was Agent Murphy. "He was a friend of my uncle's in the army. Now when he comes to the shore on business, he visits us."

"On business?" Emily repeated. She had thought of speakeasies as places in city neighborhoods—not in pretty little towns like Shell Cove. "You mean there are speakeasies around here?"

"Sure," said Gwen. "My uncle won't allow liquor in the hotel. He doesn't agree with Prohibition, but he says it's the law, so we should follow it. But lots of other places break the law. There're even speakeasies on boats, like *The Sleepy Seagull* over at the yacht club."

"*The Sleepy Seagull!*" Emily said. "That's where my sister and her friends are going tonight. Are you sure it's a speakeasy?"

"I hear guests talking about it," Gwen said knowledgeably. "It was raided once last summer, and it closed down for a while, but now it's opened up again."

For a moment, Emily was silent. It was hard to imagine that her own sister was going to a speakeasy! Finally, she asked, "What would happen if *The Sleepy Seagull* was raided again?"

"If the agents caught the owners, they'd get a big fine. Maybe jail time, too," said Gwen.

"What about the customers? *They* wouldn't get arrested, would they?"

"They might get thrown in jail for a night. The judge might fine them, too."

Emily wondered what would happen if Dorothy were arrested. What would Mother say? Dorothy might even have to spend a night in jail . . .

Suddenly, Emily thought of a way she might be able to help Dorothy—and Frank. She explained her plan to Gwen. "It's awfully risky," Gwen said.

"I have to try something," Emily insisted.

"All right," said Gwen slowly. "I guess you could tell Agent Murphy your idea. But I warn you, he's not always very nice."

Emily shrank back. "You know him. Couldn't you talk to him for me?"

Gwen shook her head. "It's your plan. You talk to him yourself," she said firmly. She steered Emily toward her uncle's office and knocked at the door. "Uncle Stuart? It's me."

A deep voice said to come in. Emily found herself in the wood-paneled office again. A tall man with red hair a few shades darker than Gwen's sat on one side of the desk.

Agent Murphy sat opposite him. Both men were puffing on pipes, and the air was hazy with smoke.

"I'm sorry to bother you, Uncle Stuart," Gwen said. "This is my friend, Emily Scott. She recognized Mr. Murphy as an agent from a picture she saw in the paper. She wants to ask him something."

Gwen nudged her forward, and Emily found herself looking into Agent Murphy's sharp brown eyes. "You recognized me, huh?" he asked. "You must have a good memory for faces."

Emily nodded, tongue-tied.

Gwen came to her rescue. "She's *very* good at it. And she can draw, too. Her mother's an art teacher. But it's her sister she wants to see you about, isn't it, Emily?"

Emily nodded again. She looked down at the floor. How could she explain her plan to this stranger?

Gwen nudged her again. "Tell him!" she whispered.

"My sister is planning to go to *The Sleepy Seagull* tonight," Emily began awkwardly, her voice barely above a whisper. "I, uh, wondered if you were going to raid it."

Agent Murphy's eyes narrowed. "Why do you want to know? So you can warn her?"

"No, sir," said Emily. She gathered her courage. "Actually, I was hoping you'd arrest her—and her friends, too. Just for a night, though. It wouldn't be any longer than that, would it?"

Agent Murphy studied her. "Is your sister keeping bad

company? Is that why you want her arrested? To teach her a lesson?"

Emily hesitated, not sure what to say.

"It's something like that," Gwen rushed in. "Please, could you help us, Mr. Murphy?"

"I'm not a nanny," the agent said gruffly. "I'm an agent of the law."

"I know, sir," said Emily, forcing herself to continue. "But if you see my sister at *The Sleepy Seagull*, couldn't you arrest her? Isn't that the law?"

The agent grunted. "I'm not telling you where we plan to go," he stated flatly. "Besides, even if I happened to run across your sister, how would I know it was her?"

Emily tried to find words to describe Dorothy, but all the adjectives she could think of—medium height, dark-haired, pretty—could apply to dozens of other girls. Then she had an idea. Borrowing a pencil and paper from Mr. Chapman, she quickly sketched Dorothy's face. She drew sketches of Frank, Bitsy, and Chadwick, too.

Agent Murphy glanced at the sketches, then nodded. "I have a pretty good memory for faces myself," he said. "If I happen to go to *The Sleepy Seagull* and I happen to see your sister, I'll know her. But, remember, I'm not making any promises."

Emily felt she'd argued as much as she could. She and Gwen left the office and rode the elevators up to the fourth floor. When they reached Gwen's room, Gwen sat on her bed and loosened her leg braces. Then she pulled out a bag of oatmeal cookies. "Mum and I made these together," she said, offering the bag to Emily. "Try some. It's getting late, and I'm hungry."

Emily glanced at the clock. It was almost ten. "Oh, no!" she exclaimed, her hand flying to her face.

"What's wrong?"

"I forgot to tell Mr. Murphy that Frank is going to leave *The Sleepy Seagull* before eleven. If he's going to raid it, he'd better go soon. Otherwise, Frank'll be gone!"

Gwen started to rebuckle her braces. "We'd better hurry," she said.

Emily looked at her friend. Gwen was obviously tired from a long day of walking with heavy braces. As much as she wanted Gwen's company, Emily knew she could go faster on her own. "I'll go by myself," Emily said. "I'll be right back."

Before Gwen could object, Emily hurried out the door. All the way down to the main floor, she practiced what she would say to Mr. Murphy. But when she arrived at Mr. Chapman's office, the hotel manager was sitting at his desk alone.

"Excuse me, sir, do you know where Mr. Murphy is?" Emily asked him.

Mr. Chapman looked up from his papers. "He just left. You might catch him by the kitchen entrance."

Emily rushed down the hallway that led to the kitchens.

There was no one by the back door. She looked outside and saw Mr. Murphy about to step into a black car waiting in the driveway.

"Mr. Murphy! Wait!" Emily called. She ran across the driveway. "Excuse me, but I forgot to tell you something," she said when she caught up with him.

"Well?" He looked impatient. "What is it?"

"My sister and her friends won't be staying very long at *The Sleepy Seagull*," Emily said breathlessly. "One of them has to be someplace by eleven o'clock."

"So you not only want me to go to this speakeasy, you're asking me to go there right away, eh?" Mr. Murphy asked sternly.

Emily looked up at Mr. Murphy's scowling face. She gathered all her courage. "Please, sir, my sister's not a bad person. But it would make all the difference if you could arrest her—just for this one night."

"I'll give you credit for persistence," Mr. Murphy said. His voice still sounded stern, but Emily saw a hint of a smile under his mustache. "Like I told you, though, I'm not promising anything." He stepped into the black car and said something to the driver. The car spun away, spitting gravel from its back wheels.

Emily was left alone in the deserted driveway. She wasn't at all sure that Mr. Murphy would help her. But she didn't know what else she could do. *Maybe Gwen will have an idea,* she thought. When she returned to

Gwen's room, however, Emily found a scribbled note on the bedspread:

Mum needed me downstairs. I'll come to your room later if I can.

Gwen

P.S. I left you some cookies.

By the note, there were three large cinnamon-scented cookies.

Emily went to her own room and carefully locked and bolted her door. Then she sat on her bed and munched absentmindedly on a cookie. It was chewy and spicy, like the ones Mr. Florio used to give her.

She thought back to Mr. Florio's cozy store, with all its tantalizing smells. Then she remembered that the whole building was now a smoky mess. Anger surged up in her. Suddenly, she was glad she'd helped set a trap for Mr. M. *I'm sorry if Frank is caught too,* she thought. *But Mr. M deserves whatever he gets. I only hope the trap works.*

The telephone on her dresser rang loudly. She cautiously picked up the heavy receiver. "Hello?"

"It's me, Gwen," a whispered voice said. "I'm in the lobby. Come down quick."

CHAPTER 15

CAUGHT!

Emily ran down the two flights of stairs to the lobby. Gwen beckoned to her. "One of the bellboys came in and said *The Sleepy Seagull*'s been raided," she announced. "Let's go outside and look."

Near the entrance, a small crowd of people were watching the road that ran between the yacht club and the hotel. In the darkness, Emily could see the lights of seven or eight cars lined up on the road. Guests gathered in groups, discussing the raid and guessing who had been caught in it. Emily saw Mr. M standing by himself, apart from the crowd. Her stomach tightened with fear. "There he is," she whispered to Gwen.

Gwen nodded. Both girls tried to slip into the darkness. Just then, however, Mrs. Brewster hurried outside. She strode over to Emily and demanded, "What's this I hear about trouble at the yacht club?"

Emily hesitated, but Gwen jumped in to answer.

"There's been a raid over at *The Sleepy Seagull*," she said, pointing to the line of cars on the road. "They're gathering up people now."

"A raid!" Mrs. Brewster repeated shrilly. She turned to the young bellboy standing nearby, as if he were somehow responsible. "Is this true?"

"Yes, ma'am," said the bellboy excitedly. "There's a bunch of agents down there. They've arrested the bartenders and the customers, too. The jail is going to be full tonight!"

"Jail! Why, that's ridiculous!" Mrs. Brewster exclaimed. "My daughter was planning to visit *The Sleepy Seagull* tonight. They can't possibly send its guests to jail."

"All I know is what I saw, ma'am," the bellboy said.

Mrs. Brewster scowled at Emily. "Am I correct? Is Bitsy over there with your sister and Chadwick and Frank?"

"Yes, Mrs. Brewster, I think so," said Emily. She paused, and out of the corner of her eye, she watched as Mr. M turned abruptly and headed back into the hotel. "That's where they were planning to go," she added.

"This is an outrage!" Mrs. Brewster declared. "Come with me. I have some telephone calls to make. And one of the first ones will be to your mother!"

Emily and Gwen exchanged a glance. "I'll see you tomorrow," Gwen whispered. "Keep your fingers crossed!"

Emily crossed her fingers in her pocket. Then she followed Mrs. Brewster up to her suite on the second

floor. She listened and waited while Mrs. Brewster
called her lawyer and Mr. Brewster. Then, after some
difficulty, Mrs. Brewster reached Mrs. Scott in
Philadelphia. Mrs. Brewster managed to imply that the
"whole wretched affair" was Dorothy's fault. Mother
promised she would catch the first train to Shell Cove
in the morning.

Clearly not satisfied, Mrs. Brewster then called the
hotel's owner, the mayor of Shell Cove, and the town's
chief of police. She pleaded and threatened, but finally
she had to accept that Bitsy, Dorothy, Chadwick, and
Frank would all be kept overnight at the Shell Cove jail.
The mayor promised they would go to court first thing
in the morning. The judge, he said, would probably order
them to pay a fine and then release them with a warning.

Finally, Mrs. Brewster gave up her attempt to have
Bitsy released. "I have a dreadful headache," she announced
to Emily. "I am going to bed."

Emily was left to find her own way up to her room.
She locked the doors carefully. Then she lay in bed and
wondered. Could the rest of her plan possibly work?

At eight the next morning, there was a loud knocking
at the door. "It's me!" Dorothy called out. "Wake up!"

Emily, still half asleep, opened the door, and her sister

entered. There were circles under Dorothy's eyes, her hair was tangled, and her silk evening gown was badly wrinkled. She glared at Emily. "I want to talk with you!"

Uh-oh, Emily thought.

"You heard about the raid at *The Sleepy Seagull,* didn't you?" Dorothy demanded.

"The whole hotel heard about it," Emily said.

"Well, when the agents went through the room, one of them came straight to our table. He looked at me and said, 'You must be the sister. You should keep out of trouble.' Then he put handcuffs on me and Bitsy and Frank and Chadwick and hauled us off to jail!"

"Oh," said Emily, trying to sound sympathetic. She was pleased that her plan had kept Dorothy and Frank safely away from the gangsters. *Now, if only I knew about Mr. M,* she thought.

Dorothy continued, her eyes blazing angrily. "I had a long night in that miserable jail to think about it. I kept wondering why that agent called me 'the sister.' It was almost as if he was looking for me in particular. Were you talking about me to some stranger? Did you tell anyone about *The Sleepy Seagull?*"

Emily fidgeted, unable to meet Dorothy's gaze. "I, uh, well . . ."

Just then there was another knock at the door. "Come in!" Dorothy said sharply, and Gwen came in.

Gwen was using her wheelchair this morning, and Emily

realized she'd probably had a long night. But she was grinning broadly. "Our plan worked!" she announced joyfully. "The Coast Guard caught them. Everybody was arrested!"

"Thank heavens," exclaimed Emily. She sat down on her bed, almost faint with relief.

Dorothy looked from Gwen to Emily. "It *was* you girls, wasn't it? You got us all arrested!"

"Yes," Gwen said cheerfully. "We were trying to help you. Your boyfriend was in big trouble—and you were, too, even though you didn't know it."

Dorothy, however, wasn't listening. "Well, that's just the limit!" she exclaimed. "My own sister turned me in! And I wasn't even doing anything. I was just sipping soda pop and listening to music!"

"You don't understand," Emily tried to explain.

"*You're* the one who doesn't understand," Dorothy exploded. "Ever since we got here, you've been cooking up crazy stories about gangsters and bootleggers. Now you get federal agents to arrest your own sister!"

"Yes, but—" Gwen began again.

Dorothy ignored her. Her voice rising, she turned toward Emily. "I hope you're happy with yourself. You've ruined our whole vacation. Bitsy's mother is furious, and we have to go home. And it's all YOUR FAULT."

"No," said a quiet voice from the hallway. "It's my fault, really."

Gwen had left the door ajar, and now Frank entered

the room. He looked tired. He was wearing a sport jacket and carrying a straw hat.

"Would you girls excuse us?" he asked Emily and Gwen. "I'd like to speak to Dorothy privately."

"You can talk in front of us," Gwen told him. "We already know about your deal with the gangster, the money you owed him, everything. Emily and I heard it all. Besides, we know something you don't. The Coast Guard arrested Mr. M this morning, along with four of his men. They were carrying over one hundred thousand dollars' worth of bootleg liquor."

Frank looked from Gwen to Emily. "You girls knew about that?" he asked, his voice betraying his amazement.

Emily nodded. "Yes."

Dorothy looked confused. "I haven't a clue what you're talking about."

Frank took the chair by the dressing table and told his part of the story. He explained that, unlike Chadwick, he didn't come from a rich family. "My parents are farmers in upstate New York," he said. "The only reason I could afford college is that I got a scholarship."

"I'm on scholarship, too," Dorothy admitted. "I never knew you were."

Frank said that he'd tried to keep up with his wealthy friends at college. He'd gone to expensive parties and had gambled at New York speakeasies.

"It wasn't too long till I started to owe money. There

was one speakeasy that let me run a tab. I was sure that all I needed was a little luck, and I'd be able to pay them back. But my luck just got worse. Finally I owed five hundred dollars, and the owners started pressuring me to pay up. They threatened to get rough if I didn't pay, but I was broke."

Frank sighed and turned over the hat he was holding in his hands. "I didn't know what to do," he confessed. "So when Chadwick invited me to sail here with him, I jumped at the chance to get out of New York. Then, the first evening we were here, I saw Mr. M in the ballroom. I'd met him before at the speakeasy, and I knew I was in trouble.

"I couldn't avoid paying the money any longer," Frank continued. "So I swallowed my pride and asked Chadwick for a loan. I didn't know how I was going to pay him back, but it seemed like my only hope."

Frank looked up at Dorothy. "I'm sorry," he said. "I never meant for you to get mixed up in any of this."

"I still don't understand," Dorothy exclaimed. She looked toward Emily and Gwen. "How did you girls get involved?"

Together, Emily and Gwen explained the rest of the story: how they'd overheard the gangster's conversation with Frank; how they'd discovered the plans for the smuggling venture; and how they had informed on Mr. M to the Coast Guard.

"But what about the raid on *The Sleepy Seagull*?" Dorothy persisted.

"That was Emily's idea," Gwen said proudly. "She didn't want Frank to go to prison for smuggling—or for you and him to be killed by gangsters. She thought the only way you'd be safe would be if you spent the night in jail."

"I guess we're even now," Frank told Emily. "I saved you once, and you saved me."

He stood up and walked toward Dorothy, taking her hand in his. "I came to say good-bye. I'm going home. I spoke with my father on the phone. He's willing to take out a loan so I can pay Chad back. I'll work on the farm till the loan's paid off."

"What about college?" Dorothy asked.

"I hope to go back in a year or so," Frank said. He smiled wryly. "Maybe I'll be smarter by then."

Frank gave Dorothy a long kiss good-bye. Then he turned toward Emily. "Remember—stay out of deep water, especially if you don't know the currents," he told her sternly. Then he smiled. "And thank you." He tipped his hat, first to Emily, then to Gwen. Then he walked out the door.

"I have to go take care of the animals," Gwen said, rolling out the door behind him. "I'll see you later, Emily."

After Gwen left, the room was quiet. Then Dorothy sat down on the bed beside her sister.

"I'm sorry, Em," she said at last. The words came out

slowly. "You were right all along, but I didn't believe you. What can I ever do to make it up to you?"

Emily thought for a while. "You can trust me some-times," she said finally. "You can believe that I'm not a complete idiot. And..."

"What else?"

"You can let me wear your new bathing suit. I really like it."

Dorothy laughed. "You can keep it," she said. "I'll even alter it so it fits you perfectly. Or if you like, I'll make you one of your own, any kind you want." Then she looked serious. "But you're not going to have much chance to wear it. Our vacation is over. Mrs. Brewster is taking Bitsy home this morning. And Mother is coming to get us."

The two sisters looked at each other. Between Emily's new haircut and Dorothy's arrest at a speakeasy, Mother was not going to be pleased.

"Uh-oh," the two girls said in unison.

◀❦▶

A taxi dropped off Mrs. Scott at the Grand Atlantic Hotel that afternoon. When she got out of the car, the girls were amazed. Mother's hair was bobbed!

"Some of my hair was singed in the fire," she explained. "I had to cut it. Now that it's short, I must admit I rather like it. It's so easy to care for!"

She looked at Emily. "I see you've discovered the same thing."

"Mother, I can explain last night," Dorothy began.

Mother nodded. "I was concerned when I received Mrs. Brewster's call," said Mother. "But you weren't hurt, were you?"

"No," said Dorothy.

"And you've learned a lesson?"

"Yes," said Dorothy. "I have."

"Then we can talk about it later," Mother said. She gave Dorothy a reassuring hug. "I'm so glad you're all right. You know, the fire was a horrible experience. I was asleep, and I had a dream about your father. He was there beside me, telling me to wake up. Then I heard Homer barking. When I opened my eyes, there was smoke everywhere."

Mrs. Scott shuddered at the memory. "Anyway, after the fire, I realized how lucky I was to be alive. I'm very thankful that we're together again, and we're all well. That's what's important."

Just then, Gwen rolled up in her wheelchair, with her uncle right behind her. As Emily introduced them, Mother looked surprised and pleased that Emily had made a new friend during the short vacation.

"How do you do?" said Mother, shaking hands with Mr. Chapman and Gwen. While the grown-ups talked, Gwen whispered to Emily, "You're not the only one who can cook up a plan."

"What do you mean?" Emily whispered back.

"You'll see," said Gwen, smiling.

Emily listened more closely to the grown-ups' conversation. Mr. Chapman told Mother that he'd heard she was an excellent art teacher. He asked if she'd consider offering summer classes at the hotel. Guests, he said, would enjoy sitting on the hotel's porches and painting pictures of the sea. In return for teaching, Mrs. Scott would be paid a small salary, and she and her daughters could live rent-free for the summer in the staff quarters.

"We've had a recent vacancy there," Mr. Chapman explained.

"Madame Serena was caught in the speakeasy raid last night," Gwen whispered to Emily. "The police say she has a record of arrests for the last five years! I guess we'll be taking care of Pauline for a long while."

Mother considered the idea for a moment. "Well," she told Mr. Chapman, "our apartment in Philadelphia is currently being repaired, so your offer comes at a good time. And this would be an ideal setting for art classes." She looked at her daughters. "What do you girls think?"

For once, Emily was the first to speak. "I think it would be wonderful, Mother," she said decisively. "We could even bring Homer. Gwen and I could take him for walks together."

Mother nodded thoughtfully. "What do you say, Dorothy?"

Emily looked at her sister anxiously. Would Dorothy be embarrassed to live in staff quarters and have Mother work at the hotel? Would she be ashamed to admit that she didn't come from a wealthy family?

Dorothy jutted out her chin with determination. "I have a concern," she said.

Uh-oh, Emily thought.

"Yes?" asked Mr. Chapman.

"I'd like to get a job, too," Dorothy said. "Do you know of any positions that might be available?"

"Well, there's currently an opening for a breakfast waitress," Mr. Chapman said. "And I know you play the piano beautifully. Perhaps you could serve as a waitress in the morning and play the piano in the lobby in the afternoon. Would that suit you?"

"That would be perfect," Dorothy agreed, smiling.

"What about Emily?" Mrs. Scott asked Dorothy. "If you and I are both working, who will watch over her?"

"Don't worry, Mother," Dorothy said confidently. "Emily can take care of herself. In fact, lately she's the one who's been taking care of me."

Mrs. Scott looked surprised. "It seems as if both my girls are growing up," she said, and she smoothed Emily's bobbed hair. "You know, I think we could have a lovely summer here."

"Oh, yes, Mother! There's so much to do," Emily agreed excitedly. She remembered all the activities she'd watched longingly from her balcony. "We could swim and go on the boardwalk and ride the carousel and eat saltwater taffy and build sand castles and—"

Dorothy laughed. "Slow down, Em. We have the whole summer."

Emily and Gwen grinned at each other. *Dorothy's right,* Emily thought. *The whole wonderful summer is ahead of us!*

1925

A Peek into the Past

LOOKING BACK: 1925

In 1925, girls like Dorothy and Emily Scott prided themselves on being "modern"—and very different from their mothers.

When their mothers were young, a woman had to wear her hair in a bun and endure corsets and ankle-length skirts. During the 1920s, however, young women called *flappers* broke free from these restrictions. They cut their hair to chin length, threw away their corsets, and wore knee-length dresses. Some daring flappers even wore pants and form-fitting bathing suits.

A flapper shows off her daringly modern bathing suit.

Girls in the 1920s had more career choices than their mothers did, too. Many parents, like Mrs. Scott, encouraged their daughters to finish high school—and even attend college. New job opportunities came as a result of the Great War, later called World War I. When men went off to Europe to fight, women temporarily took men's places in factories and offices. After the war ended in 1918 and soldiers returned home, many women were forced out of jobs, but some continued in their new careers.

In 1920, two important amendments to the Constitution went into effect. The 19th Amendment

Telephone operators working at a switchboard. In the 1920s, nearly all operators were women.

gave women *suffrage,* or the right to vote. Thanks to this amendment, girls like Emily and Dorothy were the first in American history to grow up knowing they would be able to vote. The 18th Amendment established *Prohibition*—which meant that it was illegal to buy, sell, make, or transport any alcoholic beverage, including beer, whiskey, rum, and wine.

Unlike women's suffrage, however, Prohibition didn't work. It was supposed to stop drunkenness and improve Americans' health and morals, but thousands of people ignored the law. *Bootleggers*—those who sold illegal alcohol—did a huge business. Some bootleggers made liquor in their backyards, basements, and secret factories. Others, like the fictional Mr. M, smuggled liquor into the United States from other countries.

Bootleg alcohol was often unsafe. With no government controls, bootleggers mixed all kinds of ingredients into brown bottles and sold the mixtures as liquor. During Prohibition, thousands were disabled or killed by drinking poisonous liquor.

Policemen emptying barrels of bootleg beer into the sewer

Bootleg alcohol was sold in illegal bars known as *speakeasies.* Government agents tried to shut down speakeasies by raiding them and arresting the owners and customers. One New York agent, Izzy Einstein, became so well known that speakeasies hung up his photo, warning customers to watch out for him!

Rumrunners smuggled liquor into the U.S. by land and by sea. Some coastal areas were called *Rum Rows*. The most famous Rum Row was off the New York–New Jersey coast. There, foreign ships anchored 3 miles offshore, where international waters began. As long as ships stayed out of American waters, the U.S. Coast Guard could not stop them. Smugglers in small boats sped out to the ships, bought liquor, then sped back to shore.

Coast Guard patrols had a hard time catching the smugglers' speedboats. So in 1925, when Emily's story takes place, Congress moved the international waters limit to about 12 miles offshore. This made it much more dangerous for smugglers to reach the big ships.

Still, smuggling continued. Gangsters made huge profits through bootlegging and speakeasies. In many cities, they became powerful and feared. Like Mr. M, they forced business owners to pay them money, bribed police, and threatened or

During Prohibition, foreign boats brought shipments of liquor close to U.S. waters.
Bootleggers in small boats sped out to meet them and smuggled the liquor to shore.

A police mug shot of gangster Al Capone

killed witnesses to their crimes. The most famous gangster was Al ("Scarface") Capone of Chicago. By 1925, Capone headed a gang of about 700 thugs. Other cities had their own gangs of criminals. As the crime rate soared, Americans decided Prohibition was a mistake. It was ended in 1933.

Prohibition failed, but many changes during the 1920s were for the better. The number of American homes with electricity doubled. Families bought electric washing machines, refrigerators, and vacuum cleaners. Suddenly, household chores were easier than ever before.

The radio, another new electronic device, quickly became a favorite of children and adults alike. Baseball fans throughout the country listened to games on the radio, and the slugger Babe Ruth became a national hero. A popular song, "Ain't We Got Fun," summed up the mood of the times. Fun fads swept the country. One craze was *mah-jongg,* a Chinese game played with small tiles. Women even dressed up in Chinese robes for mah-jongg parties.

Jazz became the music of the decade, and the '20s are often called the Jazz Age. The exciting music demanded a new style of dancing. Fast, athletic dances like the

Dancers doing the Charleston

Charleston were practiced in ballrooms from Boston to Los Angeles. Dance marathons, like the one Dorothy and Frank won, became a favorite form of competition. Couples struggled to stay awake and danced as long as they could move their feet.

Movies drew thousands of viewers every week. Even though there was no sound ("talkies" were not introduced until 1927), movie fans loved to watch the silent adventures of their favorite stars.

Automobiles became wildly popular. Americans loved the freedom of being able to travel wherever they wanted without depending on trains or street-

A 1926 movie poster

cars. More families could afford to buy cars because, throughout most of the 1920s, American businesses boomed and investments climbed steadily. Families like Bitsy Brewster's became wealthier than ever. Many upper-class families could afford expensive cars—and chauffeurs to drive them.

Automobiles gave a new sense of freedom to Americans who could afford them.

But while the rich got richer, laborers and small farmers, especially immigrants and African Americans, did not share in the economic boom. Many struggled to survive.

Diseases such as polio also brought suffering. People who survived polio were often permanently weakened or partly paralyzed, like Gwen. Thanks to vaccines, polio is now extremely rare in the U.S., but in the 1920s, polio affected thousands of Americans—most of them children.

Franklin D. Roosevelt

The most famous polio victim was Franklin D. Roosevelt, who later became President. After he caught the disease as a young man in 1921, his legs were paralyzed. Handsome and successful, Roosevelt changed ideas about what a handicapped person could accomplish.

Despite challenging problems such as polio and crime, the mid-1920s were a lively, hopeful time for most people. Like Emily and Dorothy, Americans were excited about living in a "modern" time and looked to the future with optimism.

AUTHOR'S NOTE

Both Emily's street in Philadelphia and Shell Cove in New Jersey are fictional. But I've been lucky enough to live in similar places in Philadelphia and on the Jersey Shore. Like Emily, I loved Philadelphia's museums. In the summer, though, there was no place I'd rather be than "down at the shore," especially if it meant I could swim in the ocean!

In researching this book, I received help from historians, librarians, and hotel staff. I'd especially like to thank Don Canney, historian for the United States Coast Guard, Jill Radel of The Museum of Yachting, and Carrie Brown, historian. I'm also grateful to artist Nancyrose Logan, who helped me to see the world as Emily might have seen it.

I owe a debt of gratitude to my husband and children for their patience, helpful comments, and continual support. Also, as I wrote this book, I remembered stories from my mother, who grew up in Philadelphia during the 1920s. She told me how, as a child, she'd been forbidden to swim in public pools because of fear of polio. She also told me how relieved she was when a polio vaccine became available and she could protect her own children from this dreaded disease.

Finally, I'd like to thank my editor, Peg Ross, who unfailingly offers both insights and encouragement. It is a privilege to work with her.

ABOUT THE AUTHOR

Sarah Masters Buckey grew up in New Jersey, where her favorite hobbies were swimming in the summer, sledding in the winter, and reading all year round. Whenever her family packed their car for vacations, her mother would include a grocery bag filled with books just for her.

As a writer, she's enjoyed living and working in different parts of the United States, including fifteen years in Texas. She and her family now live in New Hampshire. She is the author of two other History Mysteries, *The Smuggler's Treasure* and *Enemy in the Fort.*